Sinful Debts

SAN DIEGO MAFIA KINGS BOOK 1

SABLE PHILLIPS

1

ROGER

I t was too bright red to be an old stain. You only saw this color within the first hour while the blood was fresh, maybe while the victim was still conscious. I was trying not to think about the rusty, brownish color it turns after that, but it wasn't working.

I ruined my appetite by getting morbid over a plate of fries and ketchup. As I sat alone in the spacious living room, staring at my lunch and trying to forget how many bloodstains I'd seen in my life, my dad and a couple of his associates came in from the hall that led to his office. It sounded like he was making plans to go out, but when he saw me there, he stopped.

"On second thought: Roger. I have a job for you." He turned to his followers. "It looks like you two are off the hook for today. I'll be in touch." They left the room, shooting me dirty looks for depriving them of their work, like I'd done it on purpose. It wasn't often I was grateful for my dad's presence, but he distracted me from my gruesome thoughts.

"What kind of job?" I asked, setting my plate to the side.

He handed me a file folder, the kind he used for financial accounts. It was labeled *Johnson, F.*

"One of my borrowers is overdue in a big way," he explained as I flipped through the file. "I need his debt collected, one way or another." There was a glint in his black eyes that made me think he was *hoping* it might get violent. Or maybe he enjoyed forcing me to do something he knew I didn't want to do.

"Wouldn't it make more sense for you to go?" I asked. "Or Myles?" My little brother, Myles, was always eager for jobs like this; the official heir to the Moretti family "business," our older brother, had run off to live his life away from the mafia's demands, and Myles was gunning to take his place. Whether that was a *smart* idea, I wasn't so sure. Myles was reckless and selfish, not the best candidate for a leader. But better him than me; at least he wanted the job.

"I could do it myself," my dad sneered at my argument, "but it's a simple task you should be able to handle. If you're that worried, sure, take Myles along with you. I'm sure that'll make the encounter more interesting for everyone." He turned back toward his office, gesturing at the file in my hands. "All the details are in the file. Let me know when you get back."

Well, I didn't really expect to get out of it. I took a closer look at file to see what we were dealing with. Fred Johnson. Borrowed a full million from us almost ten years ago, and he'd only paid back about 75%. Terms of the loan stated he had to pay it off within nine years, so Dad was right; he was way overdue. The attached photo showed a thin, haggard middle-aged man with a mess of brown hair. Looking at him, he seemed familiar, but I couldn't remember where I'd seen him before. Maybe he'd been by the house when they were setting up the loan. It didn't change what I had to do.

I went to get Myles from his room. I pounded on the door and went in without waiting for an answer. He ignored me at first, engrossed in some first person shooter video game. Definitely the best use of his time. After a minute, he died in the game and swore, "You're throwing me off. What do you want?"

I rolled my eyes. "We've got actual work to do. Debt collection."

"Hell yeah," Myles said with a grin. "Give me a minute." I went back out into the hall to wait for him, racking my brain to figure out how I knew Fred Johnson. Why did I dread going to see him? Myles came out a few minutes later having changed out of his t-shirt and into a two-piece suit way too flashy for such a casual job. He must have been thinking my clothes were inappropriate too; as we were heading downstairs, he asked, "Is that what you're wearing?"

"What's wrong with what I'm wearing?" Sure, it wasn't Armani, but I was fine with my button-down and slacks. We would confront our debtor at a grocery story, for God's sake, and Myles was wearing fucking cashmere.

"Man, you don't get the psychological part of this at all," he said as we got to the garage. "You have to make them feel like you're better than them *on sight.* That way, you have less talking to do to prove it." Taking a set of keys out of his pocket, he dangled them in front of my face and headed toward his favorite car in the collection, a steel gray Lamborghini Huracán. He couldn't go anywhere without standing out as much as possible.

"I'm driving," I said, grabbing the keys and shoving the file at him. "Read that on the way." He groaned and collapsed in the passenger seat like a child. But when he opened the file, his eyes went wide.

"Oh, shit. Are you okay with this?" Something like worry crossed his face, a look I wasn't used to seeing on his face.

"I mean, it has to be done," I said as I started the car. "Doesn't matter how I feel." He stared at me for a minute, and I pretended not to notice, focused on my driving. We both knew I didn't enjoy this work as much as he did, but that wouldn't keep me from doing it. If this was what my family needed from me, I'd do it as often as necessary.

"Well, I can do the talking if you want," Myles said, reclining in his seat. "And if that doesn't work..." He pulled his jacket open on one side to show me his shoulder holster and the Smith & Wesson.22 strapped into it. He thought this was a fucking mobster movie, like there was going to be a shoot-out or something. One more reason he wouldn't make a good boss: he wanted the job to be more glamorous than it actually was.

"What the hell, Myles? The guy owns a grocery store. You really think you're gonna need that?"

"Will you relax? I told you, it's psychological," he said, like I was throwing a fit for no reason. "He sees this, he knows we mean business and we're not gonna take any bullshit excuses."

"So you're telling me it's not loaded?"

He sneered at the question, just like our dad when you asked him something he didn't want to answer. "You used to be cool about this." He shook his head and looked out the window. "I don't know what your problem is."

The rest of the drive passed in silence, but when we pulled up to Johnson Family Market and I got out, Myles stopped me. "I'm serious, man," he said. "If this is gonna be a problem for you—"

"I'm fine." I got out of the car before he could argue, and

he pursued. "First, we need to find the guy. His file said he's usually here supervising."

Myles snorted. "Yeah, just like our dad. It's a family business and everything."

For such a small store it was surprisingly busy. Must've been one of those grassroots operations where the service was more "personal." I wouldn't have guessed that anyone in San Diego cared about that, but there they were. We found Fred running one of the few checkout lines. Weird place for a manager and owner to be. Myles strode up to him before we could make an actual plan, leaving me no choice but to follow his lead.

"Fred Johnson?"

He looked up at the sound of his name, older but healthier than in the photo we had of him. And my feeling he was familiar got stronger when he looked at me. "Yes?"

"We have business to discuss," Myles said, arms crossed.

"Uh, I'm sorry, gentlemen, but I'm helping a customer at the moment. I'd be happy to talk with you after—"

"I think you're gonna want to talk to us now." As usual, my brother didn't know how to take "no" for an answer. He leaned forward on the counter with both hands. "We're here on behalf of our father, Deron Moretti. That name ring a bell?" Fred went pale at the sound of our dad's name, and he swallowed. The smirk on Myles's face showed how much he was enjoying this, and part of me wished I'd left him at home. I could've done this quietly on my own.

"Annette," Fred called to a girl who was stocking shelves nearby. She barely looked over eighteen. "Can you take over for me?"

"Um. Sure." There was a distinct family resemblance between them, including the dark brown eyes that watched us. Something about her, her name and her face, were familiar, too. Knowing Fred was one thing, but how could I know his daughter? Once she had taken his place at the counter, Fred led us away.

"If you'll follow me, we can talk in my office."

"No," Myles said. "Let's talk here." What the hell was he thinking? He wanted to talk, flash a gun, in front of all these people? I shot him a hard look, but he ignored me, and I couldn't weaken our position by arguing with him in front of our target. So I had to go along with it and hope he didn't get carried away.

"You know why we're here, don't you?" I asked, looking at Fred, who was trying to stay composed. "Our old man's been trying to get in touch with you for a while now, and you keep ducking him. Why is that?"

"I don't know what you mean," he said, shaking his head, getting twitchy. "We've been busy, uh, getting ready to... open our new location." As soon as he said it, regret overtook his features, and Myles barked out a laugh.

"Opening a new location! Isn't that exciting? So that's where the quarter mil you still owe us went, huh?"

"What?" said Annette, who had been listening. "I think you guys have the wrong person."

"Please." Fred's clenched his hands into tight fists, sweat beading on his forehead. "Let's discuss this in private. Let me explain, and we can come to an agreement."

"We had an agreement, Fred," Myles argued, refused to move the conversation elsewhere, displaying the power he —we—had over the situation. He took a step forward, forcing Fred toward the wall behind him. "You've had ten years, and we've been more than patient. Now it's time to pay so things won't get ugly."

"Hey! Leave him alone!" Annette started toward us, but Fred snapped at her to stay out of it.

"Listen," he said, lowering his voice, looking from Myles to me and back again. "I don't... I don't have the money right now. The expansion has been—" Myles cut him off with a loud, exaggerated sigh and turned to me.

"What did I tell you? Bullshit excuses." He reached for his gun, and I needed to act fast if I wanted to stop him from causing a panic. In two steps, I closed the distance between Fred and me, grabbing his shirtfront and shoving him hard against the wall.

"Your bad business decisions aren't our problem," I told him in a growl. "I don't give a fuck how you make it happen, but unless you want everyone to know to earn that loan, you'll get the money to us." His eyes got even wider, wild, panicked.

This was a standard condition of our dad's large-scale loans. He needed to know that if a person defaulted on their debt, he could ruin their life. Fred Johnson had been desperate enough for that money ten years ago that he'd agreed to kill a man. We had proof, proof that could destroy him—along with his entire family.

"I..." Fred's throat constricted again as he swallowed hard, his voice hoarse. "I need time. Please. I'll pay it back as soon as I can. Just give me a little more time."

"I gotta tell you, Fred, this is a pretty serious inconvenience," Myles said, jumping back into the conversation after pouting because I'd stolen his thunder. "And how are we supposed to know you'll keep your word this time? I think we'll need some collateral to make sure you follow through." With a threatening grin still plastered on his face, he strolled over to Annette and grabbed her wrist to drag her closer. "This'll do."

"No!" Fred tried to move, to help his daughter as she fought against Myles's grip, but I still held him against the wall. I didn't want to kidnap a girl who hadn't crossed us, but it had always proven to be an effective strategy with parents. I looked away from Fred so I didn't have to watch a grown man cry. "Please, no! Take me instead, leave my daughter out of this."

"Let's just go already." I could see people recording us on their cell phones, and I wanted to deck Myles for doing this in public.

"What's going on here?" Another woman's voice broke in. Maybe a bystander got involved when she saw a girl being threatened. When I looked at her, the reality was much worse. I recognized this woman. She was a teenager last time I saw her, but I still knew the wispy, mousy brown of her hair; the stubborn frown pulling on her eyebrows and the corners of her lips; the set of her shoulders in the tank top she wore. I remembered how I knew this family. Fred Johnson. Annette Johnson.

Jill Johnson. The girlfriend I'd gotten expelled from high school for.

Maybe I should have dressed better, after all.

2

JILL

"Okay. Anything else we need? You sure?" I held my phone on my shoulder with my cheek as I dug through my purse for my keys. I was running late—by my own standards, anyway. I didn't have to be at the store until 9:00 on a Sunday, but I preferred getting in by 8:30 at the latest. There was always plenty to do, problems that needed solving. I needed to handle them, to make sure things were done right.

"I'm sure, sweetheart," my dad laughed from the other side of the line as I found my keys and left my apartment. "You've been gearing up for this all month. I don't think you've missed anything."

"Oh, just wait. I'm sure there'll be *something*. I'm on my way now, okay? See you soon."

The drive between my tiny apartment in North Park and our store in Grantville was one I'd memorized by then. When we'd moved from New York, it had taken us a while to get our bearings in San Diego, but after ten years, I was pretty comfortable there. It hadn't been easy, getting the store up and running, building a customer base, establishing a reputation. But we had worked through it, and now we were about to open a second Johnson Family Market in Escondido.

When I got to the store, Dad was the only one inside, performing his usual pre-opening inventory checks despite having done the exact same check the night before. I'd tried a million times to tell him it wasn't efficient, but he always said it was better to be safe than sorry. I headed to the office to look over more job applications.

My dad might own the place, but the idea for the expansion was all mine. If I could make this store successful, it would open the door to a franchise that could spread across the whole West Coast. Meaning this one *had* to be successful. Everything needed to be perfect, from the location to the interior design to the staff. Especially the staff. And I hadn't found anyone yet that I trusted to take management duties as seriously as I did.

While I was still rereading my interview notes, my baby sister, Annette, came into the office to put her purse down and grab her nametag. "Have you picked anyone yet?" she asked, peeking over my shoulder.

"Still no."

"You know, the store can't open if there's no one to work there," she teased, and I stuck my tongue out at her.

"I just want to make sure they're the *right* ones. Opening the place and watching it fail would be worse than not opening at all."

It can't fail. I need this to work. We need this to work.

I couldn't stand the idea of my family dealing with the financial hardships we'd had in New York. I had been too young to really understand, but I remembered how it bled into our home life, how my parents were always fighting about money, how depressed my dad got. He managed to pull us through just before we moved. Even though things were better now, I couldn't shake the fear that we could end up there again.

"You worry too much," Annette said as she was pinning on her nametag, pulling me out of my thoughts. "It's gonna go great. All the people you hire will be inspired by your passion, the store will get super popular, and pretty soon we'll have people in LA begging for a Johnson Family Market. You'll be the mastermind responsible for a whole grocery store empire." Her smile as she mapped out our whole supposed future was infectious, and I couldn't help joining her.

"You forgot the part where we start seeing celebrities on a daily basis and I end up dating Chris Hemsworth." As long as we were fantasizing, we may as well get it right. Annette tossed back her head and laughed.

"Right, introduce me to Liam while you're at it." As she went to leave the office, she added slyly, "If that's what it takes for you to get a date, we'll do it."

"Jerk!" I called after her, tossing my pencil at her as she ducked out of the room, giggling. I shook my head and tried again to focus on work, her comment stuck with me the whole morning.

If that's what it takes for you to get a date.

As if I had the time. There was a reason that my thoughts of dating were all hypothetical. Plenty of reasons, actually. A fantasy couldn't distract me from my plans for the store. A fantasy couldn't break my heart. A fantasy couldn't get violent and end in blood. I kept reminding myself of all the negative the way I always did when I remembered how good it felt to be in love. That train had left the station, and I was done chasing it.

Work that day was the same as any other: train new

employees, help customers, resolve disputes, etc. One of our clerks called in sick, so Dad took over for her. Sometimes I felt he was better at the customer service side than the management side, but I couldn't tell him that. Annette must have seen me watching him from my lookout by the pharmacy.

"I think he's getting tired." She was restocking boxes of gauze and bandages. "Of management, I mean."

"Has he said that?"

"Not out loud. But he never wants to talk about the store when I visit. It seems like it just stresses him out," she explained. "I kind of think the only reason he works so hard here is because he knows it's important to *you*."

"What? It's my fault he's stressed out?" I asked, defensively. I was afraid it might be true.

"That's not what I mean. I just feel like it would be better if you took over. Officially. You're already running the place, so if Dad wanted to retire, you'd have it covered." She shrugged. I couldn't really disagree with her, but it was a moot point until Dad brought it up himself. I wasn't going to push him out of his own business if he wasn't ready to hang it up.

Before I could respond, I glanced toward the front of the store and saw a familiar face. It wasn't one of our regular customers. "Oh no," I groaned, ducking down behind the shelves by Annette's feet. "It's Brooke!"

"Why is that bad?" my sister asked in a mock-whisper..

"*Because* she's going to want more details about the Escondido location, and I don't have any more to give her!" Brooke Rodham was a friend I'd met at SDSU. I hadn't stayed long enough to finish a degree; I'd just taken a couple of business management classes there. Brooke was a Journalism major and had taken a liking to my proactive go-getter attitude. We were the sort of people who were always working, always looking for ways to get ahead professionally. We understood each other and got along well.

Four years later, I was managing the family store while she was a reporter for a local news station. She had actually helped us a lot with advertising, being a sort of small-time celebrity. Now not only did she look for ways to get ahead in her career, but ways to help us with our expansion. Sometimes she pushed a little harder than I liked.

"Hi, Annette," I heard her clear, well-enunciated voice say from over the shelves. "Where's Jill?"

"She's right here," Annette answered, pointing down at where I crouched on the ground.

"Traitor!" I hissed.

"Oh, come on, you know I would've found you anyway." Brooke stepped around the corner and looked down at me, hands on her hips. Between her glossy four-inch pumps, her elegant black updo, and her peplum decorated dress, she always made me feel a little frumpy. "Now get up and take a walk with me."

Realizing I couldn't think of a way out of it, I sighed and got to my feet. I shot a last glare at my sister as we started to walk along the back wall of the store. "All right, I know you have questions. Spit it out."

"Well, someone got up on the wrong side of the bed," she said, looking me up and down. "Are things not going well with the new place?" She'd been following our expansion progress almost as closely as I had. She knew how important it was to me.

"They're going fine," I said defensively. "How could they be going wrong when before we've even opened?"

"You tell me."

"I'm just trying to make sure we're as ready as we can be. I don't actually have any news for you."

"Oh, you might be surprised. I can find a story pretty much anywhere," she teased, holding up her hand like she had a microphone. "'Tonight on the nine o'clock news: local workaholic Jill Johnson was seen at her job wearing literally no makeup for some reason. Did she not have five minutes this morning to put on foundation and mascara? Was she so stressed that she simply forgot this step in her routine? Is this some sort of practical protest against the patriarchy and societal expectations of working women? These answers and more as the story unfolds.'"

By the time she finished, I was covering my mouth with both hands, struggling not to let her see me laugh. "Okay, I get it, you bitch. I know I look a little tired."

"You look more than tired. You're exhausted, hon. I keep telling you that you can't manage an entire franchise by yourself, and you're just going to run yourself ragged trying. Obviously you're not hearing me. Listen, it's Sunday. You guys close early today, right?" she asked.

"Yeah. Six o'clock."

"So you'll be free to come to my place around seven a share a bottle of rosé with me," she proposed brightly. "You can tell me all about the stresses of grocery store ownership and unwind and just *breathe* for a minute. Don't say no. Don't make me drink alone." She clasped her hands together, pouting pitifully at me.

"Fine, fine," I conceded, looking away, "just put away the puppy dog eyes."

"Works every time," she snickered. "Seven o'clock. Not a minute later. And I was serious: some mascara would really perk you right up." I waved her off, and she headed back to the front of the store. After a second of hesitation, I sighed and went back to the office to find some mascara and chap-stick. Apparently I was getting all sorts of helpful advice, whether I asked for it or not.

My eyes fell on the stack of manager applications again. I'd been trying to talk to Dad about them, but he kept brushing it off, saying he trusted my judgment. At the time, his comments added to the pressure I felt to make the right choice. Now I wondered if he genuinely didn't have the energy for it. Maybe Annette was right, he was tired. And if he was only working this hard for my sake, maybe I needed to let him know that it was okay to take a step back.

But if I did, that meant even more stress and responsibility would fall on me. I was having a hard time handling it already. I knew Annette wasn't interested in management. Even if she were, training her on top of all my other duties would only put more pressure on me. There wasn't a quick and easy solution to this; if there were, I would've found it already. Instead, I was still stuck in the middle of several issues, trying to piece them all together make them work with each other.

I need a vacation.

I almost laughed out loud at that. What a cute, naïve thought. Now, I needed to focus on the day's work. Then afterward, maybe I could brainstorm some solutions with Brooke.

When I stepped out of the office, I could hear a commotion at the front of the store. It was usually pretty quiet unless some senior citizen got mad about a coupon being expired, so I couldn't imagine what would have people so concerned. Whatever it was, I would do my managerial duty and resolve it.

When I got to the registers, I found that everything had come to a standstill; the clerks had stopped bagging items,

the customers had stopped shopping, and everyone's attention was directed toward the far wall. My instinct was to
scold my staff for not keeping things moving, but it seemed
like they weren't the only ones at fault. I carefully picked my
way through the crowd, trying to be as polite as possible—
until I saw what was going on.

My dad and Annette were being held against their will
by some overdressed kid and his tall friend, both struggling
to get away, both looking completely terrified. "What's going
on here?" I snapped, pushing my way toward them more
aggressively now. "Let them go! What's wrong with you?"
The two jerks looked in my direction, and I froze for a
second as I recognized one of them. His hair was a little
neater than I remembered, and the close-cut beard was new,
but I knew those dark eyes and that careless posture.

"Roger?" I could barely get his name out of my mouth.
Seeing him again brought up so many memories it made my
head spin. Memories of the years we had dated in school
flashed through my mind. It had been a progression from
feeling safe, to apprehension, ending in fear and violence at
our break up. A chill ran down my spine, but I tried to mask
it with anger. "What the hell are you doing here? Let go of
my dad." Seeming a little dazed, he did as I said. The
younger man with him sighed and let go of Annette too.

"Fine, we can take that one instead," he said with a
shrug. Annette ran to my side in tears, grabbing onto my
arm and burying her face against my shoulder. I wrapped
my arm around her and held her close, shushing her. Whatever they had done to scare her so much, I wanted to make
them pay for it. Even though Roger had let my father go he
stayed at a little distant from us.

"'That one' has a name," Roger growled. He glanced at
me, but only for a second, I thought I saw shame cross his

face briefly like a child caught being naughty. "It's been a while, Jill."

"Answer my question," I said, refusing to let him act like we knew each other. Not anymore. "Why are you here?"

"The long and short of it is that your dad owes our dad money," the other guy said, putting his hands in his pockets. "We're giving him an extension on the deadline, but we need something of his for insurance, if you get my drift." Our dad? So that meant...

"Myles?"

He grinned. "And here I was thinking you didn't remember me. Honestly, I was hoping you wouldn't have to get involved. But hey, maybe it's better this way. I'm sure you two have plenty to catch up on." He glanced at Roger, who was glaring at him, then looked back to me.

"If you think I'm going anywhere with you, you're crazy."

"We're not asking," Myles said, pulling open one side of his suit jacket to show—*holy shit*—he had a gun strapped to his side. The way he was facing, no one else must have seen it. I pushed Annette behind me.

"There's a ton of witnesses here," I said, nodding toward the crowd of shoppers, some of whom were trying to be discreet that they were listening, others were blatantly taking videos. Brooke was among the second group, and while I was a little irritated that she was making herself a spectator, I knew there wasn't much else she could do. "You're bluffing."

His smile didn't fade for a second, his wide eyes seeming a little crazed, as if the danger made this more fun for him. "You want to find out?" he asked, reaching to undo the strap holding his gun in place. "You know I can't resist a dare." Roger gripped his shoulder and looked at me again.

"Just come with us," he said. "No one has to get hurt.

We'll bring you back once your dad's debt is paid." How could he possibly think this was okay? When I knew Roger he was repulsed by his family's business and never wanted to be part of it. So why wasn't he standing up for us now? Was this some rehearsed good-cop/bad-cop routine?

"... Fine," I agreed, keeping my jaw set. I refusing to look scared. I needed to protect Annette. And whatever was going on, I was sure my dad could explain it later.

"No!" my sister wailed and clung to me, starting to sob again.

"Hey, it's gonna be fine. Everything will get sorted out, and I'll be back soon," I assured her, even though I wasn't certain of it myself.

"Please, don't do this," Dad begged, but Myles and Roger were unmoved.

"We've wasted enough time here," Myles said, checking a watch that looked like it cost more than my rent. As he started toward the door, he pointed at my dad. "You want her back, you get us our money. Last chance." Roger shook his head and stepped closer, reaching out for my arm to lead me out. I jerked away from him and marched out of the store behind Myles. The car they led me to looked insanely expensive as well, and I wondered bitterly what it must feel like to never worry about money.

"Oh, right." Myles snickered and looked me up and down as he reached the car. "Only two seats. Guess you'll have to sit in my lap."

3

ROGER

"Nice try." I tossed the keys at Myles, forcing him to look away from Jill. I wasn't about to make her share a seat with him; that smirk on his face made it obvious, I wouldn't put it past him to cop a feel. "You're driving." Despite bitching and grumbling about it, he crossed to the other side of the car and got in. I opened the door for Jill and gestured for her to get in first.

"Don't think you're going to win any brownie points just for treating me like a person," she said without looking at me. She stepped into the car and moved as far to her side as possible. The seats were wide enough that we could sit side by side, but not without her thigh and hip being pressed up tight against mine.

"Boy, you two look cozy," Myles sneered as he started the car.

Jill looked anything but cozy. She kept her arms crossed tight over her chest. Maybe she wanted to look tough, her position drew my eyes to her cleavage. I couldn't help glancing over. Fuck. Seeing her there had really thrown me and having her sitting that close wasn't making it any easier to process. I barely even knew how to talk to her after all this time. Especially after what she'd seen us do. I turned my frustration on my brother instead.

"What the fuck was that?" I demanded. "Did you not notice how many people there were watching us, or don't you care?" He shot me a cool look.

"You sure you wanna have this conversation in mixed company?" His eyes flickered to Jill, then he returned them to the road. As much as I hated to admit it, he had a point. Even if I had a history with her, she was in the same position as the rest of her family. Fighting with him in front of her would make us look weak. If there was one thing Morettis couldn't stand to be, it was weak.

Jill looked between the two of us, then shook her head in disgust. "How long am I going to have to be part of this family circus?"

"Just until your old man pays up. Could be a week, could be a couple months." Myles shrugged casually. "Any longer than that and our dad'll probably get impatient and do something drastic to get results."

"What do you mean 'something drastic'?" The tone of her voice said she didn't really want to know.

"Ah, don't worry about it. You'll probably get to keep all your fingers," he chuckled. Not for the first time that day, I wanted to fucking throttle him. "And there's always the chance he'll decide you're more trouble than you're worth and cut his losses."

She shivered slightly and chewed her lower lip turning it red. "What does my dad owe you? We haven't seen each other for years; how could he—" She stopped, and her face went blank. She was probably putting the pieces together in her head the way I had. "How can he owe you money?"

"Well, he's spent the past ten years paying it off. The

original deadline was nine, so he should be grateful we waited this long to squeeze him for it." Funny how Myles was just an open book about our operations. He really had no sense of discretion whatsoever. Even when Jill had been around the past, she hadn't been exposed to the family business. She didn't need to know the details now.

"The past ten years. Of course." She shook her head like she was lost, her arms dropping into her lap. "That's how he paid off our debts in New York. That's why we had to move. Because he borrowed money from the fucking mafia." She looked up at me with a hard glare. "Did you know about this while we were together?"

"No!" Until the point I got expelled, I had tried to pretty much ignore my dad's business altogether. I thought I could get away from it, eventually. I'd realized since then what a stupid notion that was. "I didn't even realize it was your dad until I saw you."

"Yeah, and what a difference that made," she muttered, crossing her arms again.

"I mean, to be fair, you didn't know about it either," Myles pointed out, leaning back in his seat. "Your family's on the verge of bankruptcy, then suddenly all your financial problems are solved, and you never wondered how that happened?"

She shook her head again, staring down at the floorboard. I wanted to run my hand along her back, to comfort her somehow, but I knew she'd probably slap me if I touched her. "How much does he owe you?"

"About a quarter of what we lent him. Two hundred fifty thousand," I said.

"Shit!" Shoving her fingers through her hair, she doubled over where she sat. "He borrowed *a million fucking dollars* from the fucking mafia." She sounded like she was still torn somewhere between outrage and hurt. "I can't believe he would do that without telling any of us."

"Yeah, and loans like that don't come cheap. He would have—"

"Shut up, Myles," I said, giving him a warning look. Jill was having a hard enough time hearing that her father had been lying to her ten years; she didn't need to hear that he was a murderer, too. My brother looked at me, then at her. He shrugged and turned his eyes back to the road.

"Whatever."

When we got back to the house, I wasn't sure how to handle Jill. In most cases like this, it was typical to rough someone up. We dragged them around if they wouldn't go on willingly, keep a tight hold on them so they couldn't make a break for it. But with her, I couldn't help but hesitate. Yeah, it had been a while, but I used to love this girl. I didn't like treating her like a prisoner. Luckily, she didn't make me push her. When I got out of the car, she followed me inside without arguing. The look on her face made it clear how reluctant she was. To her credit, though, she didn't cry. She didn't look afraid. Despite being pretty helpless she wasn't intimidated.

Fearless. That was the Jill I remembered. And I just kept remembering more every time I looked at her. Myles knew her too. Was he feeling the same weird familiarity I was dealing with? If so, he didn't show it in the way he treated her.

He led the way to our dad's office, where he waited for us. The room was designed to make you feel small when you stood in front of his desk, no matter who you were. He sat there across from the double doors, looking bored and apathetic, the position of a man only motivated by blood and money. That was how he *wanted* to be seen. When his black eyes fell on Jill, he frowned.

"I didn't say anything about taking hostages. Even if she is a pretty one." He sneered, and his smirk only lasted a second before he looked up at me for answers. "What happened? Let me guess: Fred doesn't have the money."

"That's what he said."

"And the girl?"

"His kid," Myles piped up, standing straight with his hands folded behind his back. He always dropped that mobster bravado shit and got serious when he was talking to Dad. If only he could do that when we were working. "We told him he'd get her back when we get our money. Seemed like the best way to make sure he pays up soon." Dad's eyes narrowed, and he looked Jill up and down. Not the way Myles did, like a perv, but like he was sizing her up as an opponent.

"You look familiar," he said. "What's your name?"

"Jill," she answered without hesitation, and he grinned.

"That's what I figured. You were the little minx who got my son expelled from high school." He leaned back in his chair and let out a derisive laugh. "And now you're here paying for your father's mistakes. Karma's a bitch, isn't it?"

"Karma?" she repeated, indignant. "I wasn't the one who—"

"No one asked you to answer," Myles said coldly. My fists clenched at my sides. I promised myself he and I would have a *talk* later. Dad just seemed entertained by his rudeness.

"Well, it looks like you'll be our guest until Fred gets me my money." Guest. Right. "Or until I get tired of waiting. We'll see which comes first. Roger, make sure Miss Johnson is nice and comfortable; she might be here a while." He dismissed us with a wave of his hand. Once we were out of the office, I led Jill toward a different wing of the house. Myles didn't come along. He probably knew I didn't want to look at him just then. She followed, but when we reached the guest room and I unlocked the door, she refused to go inside.

"I can't believe you're going along with this," she said, staring me down like I was the Scum of the Earth. "Like you think this is okay. I thought you didn't want to be a part of your dad's bullshit 'business.'"

"I am what I am. No point pretending otherwise." It was the same thing I'd told myself—and hear from my dad—plenty of times in the past. I nodded at the door. "As long as your dad cooperates, you won't have to be here long."

"You can't be serious," she insisted. "You're really locking me up like a fucking prisoner? This is the kind of person you are now? I could believe it from Myles, but I thought you were different."

"Just go inside, Jill."

"Fuck you!"

"*Please*," I ground out, "don't make me force you. I don't want to, but I will. Don't make me." The fierce anger faded off her features as she realized how serious I was. Then she stepped into the room without a word. While watching her walk toward the bed against the far wall, I remembered something. "Hang on."

"What?" She turned to face me and took a deep breath as I stepped in close. She was maybe half a foot shorter than me, always had been. As she stared up into my eyes, there was a lot going on in hers, but her shock was clear. Reaching one arm around her waist, I slid my hand into her back pocket to pull out her phone.

"You won't need this." The urge to stay close to her was a lot stronger than I expected. Muscle memory, maybe. The feeling was too familiar, the way she stared up at me, the sound of her breath... It was all too familiar. As I was leaving the room, I took one last look at her and—fuck. She *was* crying now. Because of me. Feeling like a prick but knowing there was nothing I could do for her, I shut the door to give her some privacy.

I got back to the living room and found Myles sprawled on one of the white leather armchairs, playing with the gun from his holster. "Hey," he called when he saw me, pointing the gun at me and making me tense up. He laughed out loud at the look on my face, then pointed the gun toward the ceiling and pulled the trigger. There was a dry *click* and that shit-eating grin on his face. "Told you. Psychology. Didn't expect it to work so well on you, though."

"What the fuck is wrong with you?" I strode over to the chair and shoved him onto the floor. His smile was replaced with a snarl as he scrambled up. "First you pull that stunt at the store, then you were a dick to Jill the whole time we were—"

"I knew this had something to do with her," he said, shaking his head like he was disappointed in me. "I knew as soon as I saw that file that you wouldn't be able to do this without getting messed up over her again."

"You fucking *knew* it was her family?"

"Yeah! And I didn't tell you, because I knew you'd act like this!" He was still holding the gun, gesturing with both hands. "What do you think? You two can just pick up where you left off? You think she still cares about you?"

"Shut up!" I shoved him back with both hands, and he stumbled into the wall. Like he knew what I was thinking. Like he had any idea what it felt like to see her hate me.

"I can't believe you're getting like this over some bitch you haven't seen for ten years." His voice echoed off the high ceilings. Grabbing his shirt with both hands, I shoved him harder against the wall.

"Myles, you want to fucking stop," I warned through gritted teeth.

"Or what? You'll beat the living hell out of me too?" That shocked me enough for him to get in a solid right hook, connecting with my jaw and sending me back a few steps. I didn't know what hurt more: the punch or the reminder of my past stupidity. "Maybe I should go talk to her. Maybe I'll get real close to her myself and see if that doesn't convince you she doesn't give a shit about you anymore."

"Myles, I swear to God—"

Our shouting match was interrupted when the front door opened. A man about my height with short brown hair and rectangular glasses stepped inside. His expression made it clear he was less than thrilled about being here. There was a little girl, maybe eight years old, with him. Myles and I both stared at what we thought was an impossible sight, and he found his voice before I did.

"Royce?"

The little girl's brown eyes lit up when she saw me. "Uncle Roger!"

4

JILL

I only let myself cry for a minute. I didn't have time to feel sorry for myself, but I allowed myself a few seconds to reconcile the roller coaster of emotions I'd been through within the past two hours. I imagined my dad going home and telling Mom what happened. I could just see mom and Annette crying together on the couch, helpless. Eventually, I thought about the store. Our new location was almost ready to open. Without me there to orchestrate it, I was sure that wouldn't progress either. Everything that was going well that morning was now quickly falling apart.

And Roger, that bastard! I couldn't count how many times he'd said he loved me when we were young. Apparently, he had forgotten all that, now I was nothing but another cog in the machine.

I am what I am. No point pretending otherwise.

What a cowardly, bullshit thing to say. He'd just stood there while his dad laughed at me, while his brother talked down to me, and then he'd threatened to *force* me into this room. And even after all that, when he had gotten close to me and reached around me—God, why did my heart trip over itself? Was he doing it on purpose, trying to make me feel something for him like I used to? It wouldn't work. I wouldn't let him manipulate me.

Brushing away tears of anger and frustration, I started looking around the room for any way to escape. He had taken my phone, so there was no chance of anyone else was coming to get me. I would have to get out on my own. And I *did* have to get out. These people were dangerous. I remembered when Myles was a sweet twelve-year-old. He'd been maybe a little mischievous, but not like *this*. Growing up in this environment turned him into a monster. Like his father. Like his brother.

My prison cell of a room was small, but bigger than the bedroom in my own apartment. Of course even the prison quarters in their *mansion* were better than my home. Everything was shaded in whites and cream. There was a tiny bathroom attached, stocked with towels but no soap. An empty chest of drawers. An empty closet. A twin bed, and above it, my only access to the outside world, a tiny window.

I climbed up onto the bed and tried shoving at the window. I looked for a latch or a lock, but it wasn't made to be opened. I beat on it with my fists and even the heel of my shoe, but it was no use. Even if I could break the glass, it was small, my ass might not fit through it. Definitely not without getting cut to ribbons in the process. It was just a taunting little rectangle of glass, showing me that freedom was right there, but I couldn't get to it.

"Damn it!" Refusing to give up, I marched over to the door and started pounding on it with both hands, shouting for someone to help me, to let me out. Hello? Anyone? No one? I threw a regular tantrum, shoving my shoulder against the door and screaming until my throat was raw.

Nothing. I collapsed on the floor, leaning against the

wall to catch my breath. There was really no way to escape without help. And no one was going to help me. My mind went to Roger again. He was so different from the boy I remembered. Maybe after ten years working with the mafia, being groomed as a thug, he lost all the sweetness I had loved about him before. Back then, he would never have threatened me—or anyone else, for the matter. Everyone knew his family's reputation, and when we'd met, even I was a little wary of him.

But he had proven that those preconceptions everyone had about him were wrong. Other boys our age would try to flirt with me and my friends all at the same time. They were looking for a "yes" and didn't care who it came from. Roger wasn't like that. As long as I knew him, he was only ever interested in me.

That crush of his started in seventh grade. Even then, he already had a reputation for being tough and for coming from a dangerous background. But he was never a fighter. He never sought out conflicts or responded to any of the kids who taunted or challenged him. He was kind of quiet, which a lot of people equated with brooding and unpredictable. I thought the same thing until the day I found a pink carnation waiting on my desk. I realized he was the only one who could have left it. He kept trying to sneak glances at me to see my reaction, and each time I tried to catch his eye and smile back.

Dating when you're that age is kind of a weird experience. It mostly consisted of a lot of nervously standing close together, holding hands during school functions, sitting together in class whenever we could. Eventually, there was a brief, chaste kiss followed by a lot of grinning and blushing and butterflies in my stomach. At first, I couldn't have explained why I liked him. Maybe he was just cute, or I enjoyed the attention he gave me. But as time went on, I realized how comfortable I was with him. I snuggled up against his side at the movies or joined his family for dinner. I realized that it wasn't just attention I wanted but *his* attention specifically. I loved the way he looked at me, like he was lucky to have me around.

Of course, we didn't get along all the time. We had our share of arguments—maybe more than our share, actually. I would get jealous of some other girl he was talking to, and he would have to remind me that he'd "literally never wanted to date anyone else." He would get irritated with me for not being willing to compromise on important issues, and we would argue until one of us had convinced the other. And every time, we would eventually work it out and he apologized with kisses. More than kisses, as we got older.

There was a period of about four years when we were nearly inseparable. My dad never liked him, never trusted him. Rather than him coming over to our place, I spent a lot of time at his. I got to know Myles, their older brother Royce, their dad and their step-mom, Rena. She adored me, said she was "happy to have another girl around the house." I started feeling at home around them, all of them. There were rumors about me becoming part of the mob too, that I would be brought in to The Family. Even though we suspected what sort of business the Morettis were in, it wasn't really talked about much. I thought those rumors were totally baseless. I had nothing to do with the darker side of the Moretti household—which was fine by me. And Roger wasn't interested in the subject, either. He told me he was repulsed he was by his dad's work, and he couldn't wait until graduation when he could finally get out of that house and away from the family business.

For a while, I thought Roger was the one. Somehow this

boy I had met in an English class was the boy I would marry someday. I imagined even though we would be out of the Moretti household and its dealings, we could still keep in touch with his family. That was when I thought the family and the business could be separated. When I thought Roger had the will to leave and make something more of himself.

But it hadn't worked out that way. One stupid incident that ruined all those shiny, rose-colored dreams of mine. The one time he wasn't as sweet and gentle and non-combative as usual. His dad had said that *I* was the one who got him expelled from school. He was wrong. I was barely involved. If Roger would've just talked to me...

No. Maybe there was nothing I could've done to stop it. I remembered being at lunch, sometime at the beginning of our junior year in high school. Homecoming was soon, and all my friends were talking about their dates and their dresses. My family was already deep in our financial crisis at the time, so I didn't have much to add to the conversation—but I was going with Roger, so I still looked forward to it.

Then a boy from our class ran into the cafeteria looking for me. "Jill! You need to come get Roger. He's going crazy!" I didn't know what he could be talking about. I felt concerned for Roger, so I followed him. There was a huge crowd of students filling the hall by the time I got there, and I had to shove my way through to the front. When I did, I almost wished I hadn't. Roger was there, locked in a fight with another junior, Justin Lawn. The two of them rolled across the ground, each trying to get the upper-hand, while everyone around us cheered them on.

"Roger, what are you doing?" I screamed, horrified. I had never seen him so furious, never seen him even get close to hitting anyone. He'd always been so gentle with me. It was like he'd become a different person. "Stop it!" He glanced in my direction and took a punch to the gut while distracted. Growling, he managed to shove Justin down onto his back and knelt over him, hitting him once, twice, three times— until there was blood. A lot of blood. And still he didn't stop. The encouraging shouts from the other kids had died down along with Justin's ability to fight.

"Roger..." There were tears in my eyes, spilling down my cheeks, and I couldn't keep my voice from wavering as I begged, "Please! Stop!" He looked at me again, his face already bruised, his lip bleeding, as he grasped Justin's shirt in one hand and held the other in a tight fist. Justin was nearly unconscious by that point, groaning and shifting weakly in Roger's grip.

"Why do you care so much?" he demanded. "Is it because of him? You *are* fucking him, aren't you?" It was like he'd punched me in the stomach, too. I knew there was some stupid rumor going around that Justin and I had hooked up, but I didn't think Roger would ever believe it. Didn't he know I loved him? Didn't he know I didn't want anyone but him?

"I would never," I managed, shaking my head. "I would never do that to you...!" God, there was so much blood. It smeared across his knuckles, and soaked Justin's shirt, but most of it was slowly pooling on the ground around them. He must have seen the fear in my eyes; he dropped Justin and took a step back, like he couldn't believe what he had done either. Then teachers were pushing their way through the crowd with the principal. We were ushered away from the scene. I tried to stay, to find out what would happen to Roger, and if Justin would be all right, but the teachers refused to tell me anything.

I heard Justin was in awful shape, but he would recover. Roger wasn't in class the next day. Or the next. I didn't see him for a full week, and I couldn't bring myself to try to call him. If he tried to contact me, my parents didn't tell me about it. They knew what had happened. My dad always said he was trouble to begin with. Then within a month or two, we'd moved across the country, and I had imagined I would never see him again.

We'd never had any sort of closure to our relationship. It just ended. I had wrestled with my feelings about him for years afterward, wondering if I could ever feel the same about anyone else. I wondered if I wanted to, if that level of horrible, stomach-churning violence could be born from it.

And now, there I was in his house, but God, I wished I weren't. It wasn't that I was afraid of him. Not anymore. Now I was just furious with him, for everything. And I was going to cling to that as tightly as necessary until I forgot that I ever loved him.

5

ROGER

Royce looked between me and Myles like we were kids caught fighting after school. "What are you two doing?"

"Uh, nothing," Myles said, straightening up and quickly putting his gun away so Whitney wouldn't see it. Royce preferred to keep her sheltered from the family business, even though it was inevitable she'd be exposed to it, eventually. "What are *you* doing *here*? You don't visit once in two years, and now you're just dropping in without warning?"

He had a point. Royce had practically abandoned us after his divorce. He just up and decided he didn't want to "be a part of this" anymore. Said he wanted better for his daughter. Apparently, "better" meant getting her away from our family and its influence. He forgot about his responsibilities, as if we were something he could just choose to leave. We'd all written him off as a traitor and figured he was never coming back.

He sighed and shrugged a leather duffel bag off his shoulder to drop it next to the suitcase he'd brought in. "I came back because Dad asked me to."

"Asked?" I repeated, figuring that probably wasn't the full story. Our dad never "asked" for anything. He took, or he demanded.

"Insisted," Royce agreed. He pulled Whitney close to him and ran a hand over her thick black curls while she leaned her head against him. "He was threatening Margot."

"What?" Even I had a hard time believing that. Our dad might be a ruthless bastard, but family was everything to him. I couldn't imagine him threatening the mother of Royce's child, even if they weren't together anymore. "What did he say?"

"Oh, nothing concrete. Nothing direct. You know how it works." Royce stared down into his daughter's hair, but it seemed like he was looking past her. "He just implied some things. That he 'missed' us, that the family business needed us, that it would be in everyone's best interest if Whitney and I came 'home.'"

"Motherfucker," Myles muttered, and Whitney gasped sharply. "Uh, sorry! Forget you heard that, Whits."

"Did he say what he wants?" I asked. I knelt and held out my arms to Whitney for a hug. Even after two years away, she seemed just as excited to see me as ever. She smiled brightly and ran over to hug me, nearly knocking me to the ground. "Jeez, you got so strong! You're gonna be able to beat up your Uncle Myles pretty soon." She giggled and put her fists up at Myles.

"Hear that? You better watch it, mister, or else," she teased him. Between her mom and all the time she'd spent in the UK, she had a sort of mixed accent.

"Oh yeah? I better watch it? Or else what, huh?" Myles knelt next to her and grabbed her, tickling her relentlessly while she squirmed and laughed, trying to escape. When I looked at Royce, he was smiling, but there was something sad behind it. He wanted to treat the family and the business as separate things. He wanted me and Myles in his life but not Dad. *That's not how it works.* He took his glasses off and pinched the bridge of his nose as he answered my question.

"He didn't say. I don't know if he has some sort of job for me or if it's some 'family should always stick together' bullshit." He shrugged. "My guess is that he wants me back more as an employee than as his kid. But I'm sure I'll find out for sure soon enough." He looked and sounded totally exhausted.

Part of me was glad to see him, glad to think he might be back where he belonged and I could call him my brother again. But Dad calling him back like this left a bad taste in my mouth. I didn't know where it was going. Royce didn't want to be there, and worse, it sounded like Whitney was part of the negotiations.

"You know he wouldn't really hurt Margot," I said as I got to my feet. Royce made a noise between a scoff and a laugh.

"You think?"

"He wouldn't," Myles insisted. He had his hands held up in front of him, palms out, while Whitney punched at them playfully like a boxer in training. "She's family. I mean, don't get me wrong, it was a shitty move for him to use her against you in the first place, but he wouldn't follow through on it."

"If I thought he was bluffing, I wouldn't have come back. And if you two think there's *anything* he wouldn't do to get what he wants, anything that's genuinely sacred to him, you still don't know what he's capable of." Again, his eyes got dark and distant, and Myles and I exchanged a look. I got the feeling there was something here Royce wasn't saying. The more I thought about what he suggested, the more unsettling it was; he *had* known our dad for longer than me or Myles, and growing up as the heir to the throne, he'd probably seen a lot more of the darker aspects than we had.

I didn't get the opportunity to ask what he meant. The conversation stopped as Dad walked into the room, eyes fixed on his phone. If he noticed Royce or was surprised to see him, he didn't show it. Instead, he strolled across the room to turn on the TV above the mantle. After a few seconds, he played the video from his phone. And my stomach dropped.

"If you think I'm going anywhere with you, you're crazy." Jill's voice played from the TV, along with a video obviously recorded on a cell phone. It showed me and Myles clearly as he answered.

"We're not asking." It played the moment when Myles showed her his piece, and I saw the split-second flash of fear on her face. As if I didn't already have a pit in my gut.

Dad turned his sour look on me. "I asked you to do one thing. One very simple thing. I assumed that, as my son, you'd know how to get it done efficiently, and you'd know how important discretion is in our line of work."

He gestured to the TV again, where I was telling Jill to *"just go with us."*

"And somehow, you still managed to fuck it up. How did this happen, Roger?"

I couldn't figure out why he was acting like this was my fault when Myles was the one responsible for pretty much the whole public thing. I stole a glance at my little brother, and he looked pale, nervous. At least he *knew* this was his fault. But I wasn't about to throw him under the bus, not when I knew how terrified he was of disappointing Dad.

"Things got out of hand," I said instead. "He wouldn't cooperate, so we had to do it then and there." Hopefully nobody had recorded the part of the conversation that would prove I was lying.

"And you kidnapped his daughter?" Royce asked, staring at the TV with mixed horror and disgust. Then he turned that look on me. "I can't believe you two. You stand here and talk about how important family is, but you don't bat an eye at taking someone's child as collateral for a debt." He turned to Myles and added, "You even looked like you were enjoying it."

"It's business, man," Myles muttered, but he was lacking his usual confidence, staring down at his Ferragamo oxfords. Something about the big brother tone of Royce's scolding must have gotten to him. Weirdly enough, it got to me too. Having your brother look at you with that kind of contempt can make you feel like shit real quick. "It was our only choice to—"

"Bullshit. There's always another choice. Would you say that if someone took Whitney from me? Would it just be 'business' then?" he demanded. Seeing the fear in my niece's eyes twisted my insides.

"Nice to have you back, Royce," Dad said, taking a few steps closer to him. "But let's not pretend you don't under-stand how these things work. It wasn't long ago that you would do the same, or worse, and not lose a wink of sleep over it."

"I guess it's hard to keep doing that sort of thing once you have children you care about." Royce didn't back down for a second, staring our dad down in a way Myles and I couldn't. Maybe there was a short period during my child-hood where he had gone along with Dad's directions as if he agreed with them, but it didn't last long. He met Margot when he was around nineteen, which was the point where he really started asking questions and refusing to do things he didn't agree with. Dad said that was the point when our mom's personality showed in him the most.

"That's hurtful, son. Of course I care about my children. That's the reason I'm so glad to see you; now I know Margot won't be in any danger," he said casually, ignoring Royce's sneer. Looking down at Whitney, who had come back to her dad's side, he smiled. "And of course, it's what's best for Whitney too. Now that she's under my roof, I know without a doubt that she'll be safe."

Royce spat in his face. Every muscle in my body tensed in fear for him. He knew better than anyone what our dad was capable of, what he was willing to do. And we all knew how he answered disrespect. But this time, he didn't get angry. Not visibly. He just wiped his face and chuckled darkly, taking a step back.

"You *are* my son," he said. "And you always will be. No matter how hard you try to change it." Starting toward his office again, he added, "I expect to see you all at dinner." Once he was gone, and we heard the door shut down the hall, Royce let out a slow, seething sigh.

"Daddy?" Whitney said softly, shaking his hand a little. He took a deep breath and put on a smile for her.

"It's okay, honey." He ruffled her curls. "I'm fine. Let's see if we can find your old room, okay?"

"Okay." She picked up the hot pink backpack she'd dropped as soon as they got in the door and led the way to the guest wing. Royce didn't look at us as he passed, his face stony. I worried for a second that they might run into Jill but remembered Whitney's room was on the second floor, so that wasn't likely. Even if they did, Royce wouldn't want to get involved.

"Hey..." Myles was still staring at the ground, hands in his pockets. "Uh. Thanks for..."

"Don't thank me. Just *think* before you do things." I left him there with that advice. After the way he'd acted, he didn't deserve much encouragement, and I needed a minute alone to prepare myself for dinner.

Sunday dinner together was one of the many family rituals we adhered to. It wasn't the sort of family gathering most people would imagine, though. We weren't there to bond or enjoy each other's company. We weren't meeting up and interacting out of love. It was a ceremony, a show of power on Dad's part. He could force us all together at the exact time and place he wanted, without question. I had known that since childhood. I saw how somber my usually cheerful mother would get every time we sat down at that long, dark-varnished table. That was before my mother's accident and my father's second marriage.

My dad's current wife, Rena, was fine, I guess. She wasn't awful. She wasn't remarkable. The fact that she didn't make much of an impression might have been the reason my dad liked her; she never argued when he ordered her around and was always eager to please him. Her three kids with my dad were my half-siblings, but I had a hard time thinking of them as my brothers. Royce, Myles, and I all had our mom's dark brown hair and her straight, narrow nose. Royce had her green eyes. Myles had her round face. Rena's kids looked too much like my dad. Gregorio, the oldest at nineteen, was blond like his mom. Patrick and Kurt, eighteen and sixteen respectively, were like mini copies of Dad with his black hair and eyes. One of him was plenty. We all grew up together, more or less, but there was still distance between us and them that I couldn't get past.

When we gathered in the dining room as usual, Rena's whole face lit up when she saw Royce and Whitney. She swooped in on them with hugs and kisses, either ignoring or oblivious to their awkward stiffness. Dad soon told her that was enough, and she stopped without argument, taking her seat next to him. The table divided the two sides of our family, with Rena and her boys on one side, me and my brothers on the other. Myles had changed his clothes again into something more understated which matched the gloomy atmosphere of the room. Dad preferred that for our family meals.

The house staff served dinner, Cioppino and garlic bread, but even the intense smells of seafood and tomato seemed muted. While we were eating, Rena was the only one immune to the oppressive mood. She gabbed on and on about the shopping and sewing she'd done that day. Patrick's upcoming high school graduation. How big Whitney was getting. Nothing really worth hearing.

Royce didn't say a word the whole time. It looked like he barely ate. Was he that miserable? I stole a look at Dad, who seemed like he didn't even notice Royce's bad mood. What the fuck did he care if his son was unhappy, as long as he was doing what he was told? He was the same with me and Myles. The same with his wife. Just follow directions and all is well. *Bastard.*

I drained the rest of my wine and put my glass down too hard, clanging it against the table and drawing everyone's attention to me. I needed an excuse to leave before my temper got the best of me. "Can I be excused?" I asked through gritted teeth. "Our 'guest' is probably hungry." Dad stared at me for a second, then waved me off.

"Fine."

On my way to the kitchen, I wondered if this was an excuse to get away from him or to see Jill. After one of the new girls, a redhead who had a hard time making eye contact, made a plate for me to take to her, I stepped out into the hallway to find Myles there waiting for me.

"Tell Jill I said hi," he said as he passed. Then he called after me, "Hang on. If you... ugh. If you get a chance, you should try to talk to Royce. I feel like if I try, I'll just irritate him, but he might actually listen to you. Just. See if he's okay." He shrugged and headed for his room. He looked embarrassed that he showed any concern for someone other than himself.

Talk to Jill. Talk to Royce. Try to find and destroy that video Dad had showed us earlier. It looked like it would be a busy night for me.

6

JILL

I expected the Morettis to torture me, but I didn't think it would happen like this. Sitting alone in this room for hours was going to drive me crazy. Was that their plan? Solitary confinement until I lost the will to fight? Well, I wouldn't. There wasn't even a clock, so I couldn't tell how long it had been. I could see through my little window that the sun had mostly set. An hour or two ago, I'd heard some shouting from the living room, but I couldn't tell what was being said. Every once in a while, I would hear a voice or footsteps, and I would repeat my pounding on the door and shouting for help routine. It never worked. No one ever came to my rescue.

Sometime after dark, as I was lying in my bed and staring up at the ceiling, wracking my exhausted brain for a solution to this, I heard footsteps again. I started to get up and go to the door, but it opened before I could get there. Roger appeared in the doorway, carrying a tray with a bowl of soup and some bread. As soon as I smelled it, my stomach cramped to remind me how hungry I was. Italian food sounded *amazing* at that moment. But I refused to let him see that I was grateful. He set the food down on the dresser and turned to leave without a word, without even looking at me, and I spoke despite myself.

"Wait." He paused in the doorway, still not looking at me. "Would you tell me what's going on out there? Give me some kind of update?" A moment passed in silence. "After everything you've done, that's the least you owe me." His shoulders slumped, his head dropped, and he finally turned around to face me, pulling the door closed behind him. So I wouldn't try to escape, I guess.

"There's not much to tell." He leaned back against the door, arms crossed, and every few seconds his eyes would flit to me, then away again. I watched his body language for any information it might give away, desperate for anything that might help me get out of there. "... You remember Royce?"

"Of course." Roger's older brother, Royce, had always seemed a little subdued compared to the rest of their family, not quite as confident. But he was kind, the sort of big brother I would've wanted.

"He left us for a while. Moved to the UK. Bristol, I think. We didn't hear from him for two years. And then he showed up tonight." It seemed like he was in shock. I would have thought most people would probably be excited to see a sibling that had been MIA for two years, but things with this family were never that simple. Obviously.

"You don't seem happy about it, though," I pointed out. I didn't know why I was attempting to play therapist. But, if it made him more sympathetic toward me, it was worth a try. "Why is that?"

"He didn't come back because he wanted to. He came back because our dad forced him to." His gaze got harder, and I could see a sneer starting to form in the corner of his mouth. "And it's so obvious he doesn't want to be here. He doesn't want Whitney around us, either."

"Who?"

"His daughter. She's eight years old, and she doesn't belong in"—he gestured vaguely at the house — "This." Eight years old? If Roger and I had stayed together just a little longer, I might have gotten to meet her. I knew hypothetical what-ifs like that didn't do anyone any good, but I'd be lying if I said I hadn't thought of it before. More than once. After all those times I'd imagined us growing up and getting married, it was a tough habit to break.

"Neither do I," I told him. His eyebrows jumped up in surprise, but he quickly scowled and turned away. "You know I'm right, Roger. I wasn't involved whatever business my dad did with yours. I'm not at fault here. I don't deserve to be held captive because of it."

"Maybe not," he agreed, and I almost felt hopeful, "but it's happening, anyway. This is how the world is. Sometimes innocent people pay for the mistakes of others. It's not fair, it's not right, but it's the way things are, and I can't do anything about it."

"What happened to you?" I got up from the bed and came to meet him, to glare up into his dark eyes. "Since when do you subscribe to this bullshit 'I am what I am,' 'that's the way things are' philosophy? When did you give up?"

"Give up what?" He shifted uncomfortably and backed up closer against the door.

"Your choices. Your future. In high school, you couldn't have cared less about your family's business," I reminded him. I wasn't sure if this would help my case, but either way, I was sick and tired of listening to his defeatist crap. "In fact, you made an effort to get away from it. What happened? What changed?"

"You know exactly what happened! You were there. You saw what I was. I had that violence in me. I felt threatened, and that's how it came out." His hands clenched into fists at his sides, but he didn't make any move to advance on me, to push me back. "What happened to me? I grew up, and I understand the world better now. You're here because you wanted to keep your sister safe, aren't you? Well, I'm here because my family needs *me*. I'm not going to run away from that."

"So staying loyal to your family is more important than other people's lives? Is that what you think?" I wasn't buying it. None of it. He could pretend it was realism or maturity all he wanted, but that didn't change what it really was: cowardice. "You know, I really thought you cared about me back then. I thought that was real."

"It was," he said immediately, his voice low and rough. His eyes snapped down to my lips, then up to meet mine again, and I knew I was getting to him.

"It's a little hard to believe that. Because now it seems like the only thing you care about is doing what your father expects of you." I leaned in closer, dropping my voice to match his. "That boy I knew in high school? The one who said he loved me? He didn't give a shit about his dad's approval, and he would know this is wrong. If those feelings were ever real, you would prove it now and help me."

My fingertips touched his chest, and his resolve broke. His arms snaked around my waist, tightly this time, and pulled me into him. When he leaned down and kissed me, my mind was torn over what to do—but my body wasn't. I kissed him back reflexively, grasping at his shirt with both hands, letting his tongue tease my lower lip, then slip inside to explore.

He tasted like red wine, rich and dark, and hotter than I remembered. It was distantly familiar and lit a fire in my lower belly. One of his hands found its way into my hair, in spite of being furious with him and to hating the idea of revisiting my old feelings, my mouth still knew his, and my physical memories were harder to control.

Just as I started to slide my arms around his neck, he broke away from me to catch his breath, his eyes unfocused and, I realized, staring down my shirt. "I..." His voice was hoarse, but he shook his head and put his hands on my arms pushing me back. "I can't." He fumbled a little with the lock on the door, then quickly disappeared out of it, leaving me to shiver from the sudden loss of his body heat.

God. What the hell did I just do?

Realizing my knees had gotten weak, I went back to sit on the bed and pushed my hair back with both hands to try to calm myself down. Roger had definitely grown up in the time we'd spent apart, but not the way he said. He held me the same way he had when we were sixteen, sneaking behind the bleachers to make out. He kissed me the same way he had the first time we made love. Another memory I'd revisited time and again over the years.

It didn't happen in the back of his car or upstairs during a party. It wasn't a casual, quick and dirty thing, because he wanted it to be perfect. I wasn't so picky about the setting. We wanted each other like crazy, but he insisted it was important. He wanted it to be perfect for me. Underneath that leather-jacketed bad boy exterior, he was so much sweeter than anyone else knew. He was back then, at least.

He somehow managed to orchestrate a night when his parents and his brothers would be out of the house. Just us, his bed, our privacy. Like he said: perfect. He took his time undressing me, said he didn't want to rush, and he kissed nearly every inch of my body before we finally did it. By the clumsy way he handled the condom and the awe in his eyes every time he looked at me, I guessed he was a little nervous too, which was reassuring.

It took a little time, but we figured it out together. It was hard for me at the beginning, but he was sure to go slow, breathlessly telling me I was beautiful, covering my neck and breasts with kisses. Our timing was a little off, and he came before me—but after, he wanted to make sure I did too; lying at my side, he slipped his hand between my legs and took instructions on how to touch me until I came too, overwhelmed and almost tearful from loving him so much. He told me he loved me, that I was perfect. He kissed me, and I believed every word.

And the way he'd kissed me all those years ago was the same way he had kissed me just now. My fingertips absently found my lips. Did he still feel that way? Did he still love me? Maybe it wasn't hard to believe. And I felt only a very slight niggle of guilt as I realized I could use that to get out of here.

7

ROGER

uck. Fuck!

When I left Jill's room, I had to take a few slow, deep breaths to clear my head. What was wrong with me? The way she was talking, getting so close to me like that... I was already having a hard time keeping myself in check. Then she touched me, talking about proving my feelings, and I acted before I could think to stop. Shit. And it was only worse because it felt so damn good.

She still fit in my arms perfectly. Still melted into my body when I pulled her close. Her kisses were bold as always, almost aggressive. I swore when I traced her spine, she moaned for me. For me? That was the weirdest part: how eager she had been. After everything that had happened between us that day, she acted like she hated my guts. Then when I kissed her, it was like... like we both remembered everything all at once. And she must have made a powerful impression on my memory, because just those few kisses had sent the blood rushing between my legs like I was sixteen again.

No. No matter how much I wanted her, staying in that

room would only be trouble. For everyone. Would sleeping with her count as "fraternizing with the enemy"? It wasn't as if being with her long-term was viable; she would leave as soon as we let her and never look back. *No. Forget about it. Forget it happened.*

Once I was calm enough to walk straight, I wandered down the hall, lost in my memories. Just like I thought, everything about her was too familiar. And now that I'd kissed her, I couldn't stop thinking about all the times we had kissed before. All the times she'd smiled at me, said my name, told me she loved me—only now, I could imagine it in present tense with her adult self. My imagination was too vivid. I thought of her sliding her hand up my thigh under the table in the library. That little wink she gave me afterward. The few times I'd had her in my bed.

No, that territory was too dangerous. I shook my head and headed for my room, desperate to be alone to try to forget all this or take care of it some other way. I saw Myles in the hall, and he grabbed my arm as I passed.

"Hey, so, we're internet-famous now," he laughed nervously. I forced myself to focus and understand what he was talking about.

"Huh?"

"That video of us at the grocery store earlier. Our whole little, uh, performance," he explained, hands in his pockets. "It kind of blew up. Went viral. It's all over Twitter, and people are talking about looking for Jill. It's a bigger deal than I thought it would be." I didn't even have the energy to be worried about it, too distracted to think about exactly what this could mean for us.

"It's already done, I guess," I told him with a shrug. "That's what happens when you spend your entire life as a criminal. Sooner or later you get caught, and you have to pay for what you've done. Maybe it's 'sooner' for us rather than 'later.'"

Myles leaned back and stared at me in wide-eyed confusion. "Man, you're fucking depressing. I was gonna say 'don't worry about it.' This kind of thing has happened before, and we always get out of it. Our name is all we need to make it go away." He leaned down, trying to catch my eye. "What's up with you? Is it about Jill? Did you two talk?" I also didn't have the energy to deal with his prying. I shook my head and walked past him without answering.

"I'm telling you, Roger," he called after me, "She's bad for you." Flipping him off over my shoulder, I kept walking.

Something was up with me, that was for goddamn sure. It was getting late, and I dropped myself into bed to kick my shoes off. Maybe I just needed sleep. Maybe that would do something for the thoughts that were taking over my head, making it impossible to focus on anything else.

She was right when she said she didn't belong here. It *was* bullshit for her to take the fall for her dad's problems. But what the hell was I supposed to do? Just let her go? Like that would help? Like if I did, my dad wouldn't be after hers anymore? That wouldn't work. That wouldn't fix anything. But I was sure she didn't want to hear that; the way she saw things, there was right and there was wrong, and I was choosing to do wrong. As if I had a choice about anything. She'd always been black-and-white like that, even in high school.

"Either you agree with me or you don't."

"Either you're friends or you're not."

"Either she's lying, or she isn't. There's no halfway."

And she usually assumed whichever option was worse. But then, she would try to make it better.

"If we don't agree, we're not understanding each other well enough."

"If you're not friends, it doesn't matter anymore that he's mad. If you are, then apologize."

"If she was lying, there must have been a reason. What is she afraid to say?"

Was she still like that? Still willing to improve a bad situation if she could? Or had she decided that things—and people—that were "wrong" weren't worth her time? It was stupid to even be wondering all this, since I was positive she'd decided *I* wasn't worth her time. But if that was the case, why the hell did she kiss me so hard?

For a while, I kept trying to sleep. My mind kept coming back to her. It seemed like there was only one way to make it stop. It was around 11:30 when I got out of bed and tried to make my way downstairs quietly. I was just going to talk to her, I told myself. That was all I was looking for. Answers. Maybe to find out if she was thinking the same sort of thing I was. And if she wound up kissing me again, I would definitely have the willpower to tell her no.

Definitely.

Since it was so late, and the light was off, I stopped outside her door and knocked quietly. I heard a gasp from inside. "Jill? It's Roger." Why was my mouth so dry? "Can I come in?" After a few seconds, she answered, her voice a little shaky.

"Y-yeah."

I unlocked the door and stepped inside, turning on the lamp by the dresser instead of the overhead light. Closing the door behind me, I glanced over at Jill. And I could tell something was up. She was sitting on the edge of the bed, arms and legs crossed tight. The covers were mussed, and so was her hair.

"What do you want?" she asked. Glaring at me hard, she seemed to be trying to regulate her breathing, every deep inhale drawing my eyes back to her chest. The way her arms pushed her tits up and together, I could see she wasn't wearing a bra—in fact, it was lying on the ground by the bed. When she noticed where my eyes went, she let out a squeal of embarrassment and grabbed it up, shoving it under the covers. "*What* do you want?"

Holy shit.

"Were you...?" I didn't even know how to finish the sentence. How do you casually ask a girl if she was getting herself off before you came in the room?

"Was I what?" she challenged. Damp hair stuck to the back of her neck with sweat, and she squirmed a little where she sat. "If you don't have anything to say, go away."

"Were you touching yourself?" I forced myself to say it, and she immediately turned away from me, hunching over a little more in embarrassment. After a second, she let out a soft laugh.

"That was a hell of a kiss earlier," she confessed. The way she looked me up and down, then finally met my eyes set my blood on fire. When she licked her lips, all that heat went straight to my cock. Leaning back on her hands, she tossed her hair back over her shoulders. "So? Either you're gonna stay or—"

Because the room was so small, it only took a couple steps for me to meet her at the bed, and I was kissing her before she could finish the sentence. Her mouth met mine just as eagerly as before, letting me inside, playing with my tongue. She was in here getting herself off, thinking about kissing me, thinking exactly the same things I was. I groaned against her lips and pulled her up into my lap so she was straddling my legs. My hands slid up her ribs to grope her through her shirt, and she pulled away from me to moan, "Take it off." I was already at a point where I couldn't even start to argue with her, so I slid my hands under her tank top and pushed it off over her head.

I only took a split-second to look at her, too impatient to keep going. My lips and tongue worked down her neck while her fingers slid through my hair. Every sigh out of her mouth, every twitch and gasp just made me want her more. Sliding one hand under her ass, I pushed her up onto her knees so my mouth could reach her chest. My tongue slid over one of her nipples, and she used her grasp in my hair to hold me closer while I sucked.

"God," she breathed, tilting her head back. I didn't know how much experience she'd had since our last time together, but it seemed like she was as sensitive as ever. Her hands worked quickly at the buttons of my shirt and pushed it off my shoulders so I could toss it away. Then she shoved me down onto my back and kissed me again, even harder than before.

Her jeans were already unbuttoned, and her breath hitched when I unzipped them and slid my hand down the front of them. Even through her panties, she was so fucking hot. I pushed them to the side so my fingertips could explore the slick heat of her pussy, and she dropped her head to the bed next to mine.

"Shit..." With Jill clinging to my shoulders, letting out high-pitched moans and whimpers into my ear, pressing her hips down against my hand to help me out, I was so hard my pants were really becoming a problem. Trying to get her impatient for the real deal, I pushed two fingers inside her, and the moan she let out was deep, satisfied.

"Slow down or I... won't last much longer," she panted

when I went back to teasing her clit. I could practically feel the heat coming off her cheeks.

"Oh yeah?" I asked, smirking.

"Shut up," she mumbled. "I got a head start."

"If you want, you can lay down so I can do this right," I suggested, making sure I touched her slower so she wouldn't get too far ahead of me. "That way, I can probably catch up." She let out a little laugh and kissed me again, then climbed out of my lap. I sat up in time to see her push her jeans down and off, giving me an amazing view of her ass and how wet she was. When she saw me staring, she must have realized how it looked. She looked a little shy and crawled back onto the bed, leaning forward to run her tongue along the shape of my ear.

"Well, what are you waiting for?" she asked, unfastening my pants so slow it felt like torture. "Show me you still know how to do this right." I wasn't sure if that was a challenge or an invitation, but either way, I planned to meet it.

8

JILL

Roger didn't need to be told twice. I lay down on my back, stretching out so he could see every inch of me, hoping he liked what he saw. He swallowed hard, and maybe I liked that I could still have this effect on him. After stripping out of his clothes and settling between my legs, he leaned over me—then stopped abruptly.

"Shit," he muttered. "I don't have a condom or anything." Oh. I'd gotten so worked up kissing him earlier, then when he'd caught me with my hand down my pants, it got me even more excited, even more frazzled. I'd been so busy acting on old instincts that I hadn't even thought about this part. Biting my lip nervously, I debated my options but quickly decided I was too impatient to keep waiting.

"I'm on birth control," I told him, positive he could see how dark I was blushing. "So don't worry about it. I don't want to stop."

"You sure?"

"Roger!" I insisted, letting a desperate whine sneak into my voice, and he laughed, sending chills down my spine. He lifted my hips up to his, sliding his cock against me, and I shivered just from that. "Don't keep me waiting."

"Have you always been this pushy?" he laughed. Before I could answer, he leaned forward and started to press inside me, stealing my breath. He let out a huff, too, resting over me on one hand and slowly rocking his hips to get deeper, letting me gradually adjust to him. *So sweet...* No! I couldn't be thinking about that right now. I needed to remember why I was doing this, that it could lead to him helping me escape. But God, when his hips were flush with mine and he was fully buried inside me, my eyes did go a little blurry. Well, there was no reason I couldn't enjoy it, right? It had been a while since I'd done anything like this, but just like the kisses, just like his arms around my waist, our bodies seemed to still know each other.

"Mm, don't stop now," I breathed, holding onto his hands where they rested on my hips. The softness in his eyes said this was getting to him too, and not just physically. He pulled back, still going slow, then thrust back in so my body jumped and I moaned out loud. God, he was good, and he'd barely started! Once he knew I was comfortable and practically begging for it, he started up a rhythm, slow at first, and I couldn't have kept my voice down if I'd wanted to. He would ask me now and then if I was okay, and I kept having to reassure him that I could handle it, that I wanted it, that he needed to *give it to me* before I lost my mind. The whole time he was fucking me, my body was on fire; I'd already gotten close earlier, so he was just pushing me harder and harder and harder.

Did I want this to be as familiar as it was? Did I want to feel so close to him while we were doing this? Whether I wanted to or not, whether I meant to or not, I *did* feel it, and I couldn't pretend not to. The sound of his voice wasn't helping me keep my distance either, the sighs and groans he let out, the way he'd pause deep inside me to line my neck with kisses and tell me I was beautiful. Why couldn't he be like the other men I'd been with and be selfish the whole time? Why couldn't he ignore me and act like there was nothing emotional between us at all? That would've made it so much easier for me to pretend too.

"Jill..." He was leaning in too close to me, his voice in my ear. "I'm getting close. Can I...?" He left the question open-ended, so it took me a second to realize he was asking if he could cum inside me. I had never let anyone, never wanted it or trusted anyone enough for that before. But in this moment, the last thing I wanted was for him to put distance between us, even for a minute.

"Yes," I managed, despite the weakness in my voice. "Yes. Just don't stop." Raising one hand to my lips, I licked my fingertips wet and slipped them down between my legs to touch myself. Roger groaned as I got tighter, but he only went faster. When I was already so worked up and he was doing *everything* right, it only took a few seconds of my fingers sliding wetly against my clit until I came for him. And I made sure he knew it, arching my back, calling out his name. His hips clashed against mine one more time, rough, and I took in a sharp gasp as heat flooded through me in a way I'd never felt. I hadn't considered what it would actually feel like... but it *did* make me feel closer to him, and I wrapped my arms around his shoulders to hold him tight against me.

"God..." was all I could get out as I struggled to catch my breath. He let out another brief laugh.

"Tell me about it." The bed wasn't intended for two people, so when he collapsed at my side, we were forced to stay close. Not that I minded. I curled up against his chest, and he wrapped his arm around my shoulders like it was the most natural thing in the world. It seemed like that kiss earlier had been a trip down Memory Lane for both of us. My eyes wandered slowly up his stomach to his chest, along the defined shape of his shoulders, up to his stubble-covered jaw. Then my eyes met his, and I realized he had been looking me over too.

"We never got to talk before," he said, rubbing his thumb slowly against my shoulder. "Before your family moved out here."

"You mean after what happened at the school. With Justin."

Roger's eyes snapped away from mine and up to the ceiling. "Yeah."

"I remember. It was like you just disappeared off the face of the Earth." Yes, I remembered that period of crying myself to sleep every night for weeks. When we stopped talking altogether, even though neither of us had said it, I'd assumed our relationship was over. How could I have justified continuing it after what he did? How could I have pretended that was okay?

"I was too ashamed to even try getting in touch," he confessed. "Like I had no right to try to talk to you. I'm. I'm sorry I put you through that. All of it." The remorse in his voice was painfully obvious, and I struggled with my next question before I could ask it.

"Did you really think I slept with him?" It came out more quietly than I intended, embarrassingly fragile. It shouldn't even matter to me anymore.

"No," he said firmly. "Every time I heard someone say it, it pissed me off, but only for your sake. There was something about that day, when Justin started talking shit himself. I don't know if he was trying to look tough by fighting me or what, but he was saying all this disgusting, disrespectful shit about you." He gripped my shoulder a little tighter. "I couldn't handle it. I just saw red, and I couldn't think straight. I didn't mean for it to go as far as it did—but that doesn't change what happened. Which is the reason I didn't try to explain myself to you; nothing I could say would make it any better."

"So you got expelled," I said, thinking of what his dad had mentioned earlier, "And then...? Did you enroll some-where else to graduate?"

"Nah." He shrugged vaguely, seeming a little embar-rassed about this subject too. "Just started working for my dad right away. He could've paid the school and Justin's family off so I could go back. But he didn't. He said it was a matter of time before I lost my temper again and actually killed someone; might as well be someone who deserved it."

"My God." I couldn't help recoiling a little in shock, but he hardly seemed to notice, like his mind was elsewhere. His face was set in a dark scowl as he continued to stare up at the ceiling. "Roger, that's horrible. You didn't believe him, did you? You were young, and you only got violent because Justin provoked you. That's not the kind of person you are."

"I don't know what makes you say that." His tone had gotten sort of apathetic, like this was a topic he'd thought about plenty of times and he'd always come to the same conclusion. "It's how I was raised to be. It's pretty much all I ever saw growing up. How else could I have turned out?"

Again, he just seemed resigned to what his life had become. He didn't embrace it like Myles. He didn't resist it like Royce. Passively, he let it happen because he didn't know what else to do. Had his dad brainwashed him so thor-oughly that he genuinely believed this was all he was capable of?

"There's always another choice." I knew his eyes were on me without looking. I hoped my words would get through to him. But he didn't say anything in response, and it was impossible to tell what he was thinking based on his expression.

The sticky feeling between my legs was beginning to make me uncomfortable, so I hurried off to use the bathroom. When I came back, I half-expected Roger to be gone —half-*hoped* he would be gone so I could have some time alone to think—but he was still there in bed. He'd put his boxers back on but seemed like he was waiting for me to come and continue our conversation. Wishing I had fresh clothes to change into, I grabbed my panties and shirt and put them back on before crawling into the bed, this time leaving a little distance between us.

"It kind of surprises me that we both ended up here," I said, lying on my stomach, resting my head against my hand. So weirdly casual, weirdly natural. "When did you guys move from New York? You weren't following us, were you?"

"No. I mean, I don't think so, anyway. Rena was originally from California, remember?"

"I didn't know that." She had always been much more inclined to talk about the rest of the family than herself. I didn't know a lot about her life before she'd married into the Morettis.

"Yeah, she grew up in L.A. I think her dad moved them to New York so he could run for some political office." Roger shrugged, seeming bored by the subject. He and Rena had never been especially close, but his attitude toward her was almost pointedly disinterested, like he wanted to make it clear she could never replace his mom. "Anyway, she always hated how cold it was there. Maybe

Dad got tired of hearing her talk about it after a while. Can't blame him for that."

"What about her irritates you so much?" I asked. "She was always perfectly nice when I knew her, but you were still sort of cold toward her then." I couldn't remember Royce or Myles ever treating her that way. Had she done something to Roger to earn his resentment? When I mentioned the subject, an irritated frown tugged down his mouth.

"Do I have a reason to be buddy-buddy with her? She's just my dad's wife." Did that mean he rejected the step-*mother*, idea altogether?

"Roger, she's been a huge part of your life for... what, twenty years now?"

"Almost."

"You can't act like she didn't help raise you. And you still don't feel any kind of emotional connection to her?" I wasn't sure why this was bothering me so much now, but it really was. I'd always been so close to my parents, but it seemed like there was a huge distance between Roger and his. How was he just okay with that?

"What does it even matter?" There was a definite edge to his voice by then. "I don't have any obligation to be close with her."

My eyes wandered away from his and down to my pillow. Why was this such an issue for him? Was he so stubbornly afraid of betraying his mom's memory somehow that he couldn't acknowledge everything Rena had done for him and his brothers? Was this another one of those unexplainable Moretti loyalty deals? The logic was hard to follow.

Roger brought me out of my reverie by climbing over me to get out of bed. Without a word, he started re-dressing himself. Was bringing up his mother's death such a mistake that he would no longer speak to me because of it? And more importantly: was this the end of our conversation altogether?

"So what did you come down here for in the first place?" I asked coolly, sitting up and drawing my knees up to my chest. "I don't think it was because you decided to let me go."

He sighed as he shrugged his shirt back on. "You know I can't do that."

"But fucking me is totally fine?" I glared at him as hard as I could, hoping he would feel it and it would *hurt*. "Is that what this is now? I'm locked up in here so you can come have sex with me whenever you feel like it? Is this how you treat all your prisoners?"

"I just came down here to talk," he insisted, now fully dressed and turning to look at me. "*You* were the one who offered!"

"Oh, as if you weren't thinking about it," I snapped. "As if you really came to my room at fucking midnight 'just to talk.' If you're going to use me for sex, at least have the decency to be honest about it."

"I wasn't using you." He actually seemed hurt by that, and as much as I wanted it to feel satisfied, it only made me feel guilty. "Yeah, I wanted to sleep with you. But I only acted on it because it seemed like you wanted it too."

"And that's the end of it. We'll just do it, and you think I'll forget that you're keeping me here against my will?" This was the reason I couldn't let myself remember loving him. This was why, no matter what I felt when I was in his arms, I couldn't trust him.

"Jill, I *want* to help you. If it was up to me, I would let you go. But my dad needs—"

"Spare me your broody weight-of-the-crown bullshit," I

said, rolling my eyes. "I'm so tired of hearing about how your family 'needs' you to be this way. You're not here because they need you. You're not here because it's where you belong. You're here because you're too much of a coward to try to be anything else." There was tension building in his shoulders, his hands clenching into fists, but I didn't stop. "And that makes you worse than anyone else here! Because you could be so much better, you *want* to be, but you're too lazy or too scared to try!" He turned and started toward the door in the middle of my attack.

"Roger!" I called after him, but it didn't stop him from unlocking the door and stepping out without another word. Grabbing one of my shoes from the floor by the bed, I hurled it at the door and shouted, "Bastard!" I didn't care if I woke the entire house. No answer came from the hall. Just silence. I collapsed, exhausted and furious, with my face in my hands, and tried in vain to hold back the tears. It was no use. My mind was too cluttered, too distraught to keep compartmentalizing everything and staying calm. So I let myself have the time to cry now, my shoulders shaking with unrestrained sobs.

Why did he have to come back into my life? This day was going so well, everything was moving forward just the way I planned, until *he* came along and brought it all screeching to a halt. And he had the nerve to act like he still cared about me. He had the audacity to kiss me like he knew me, to hold me gently, to make love to me so perfectly...

"Damn it." I knew I shouldn't be thinking about him like that. I wanted so desperately to cling to my anger, to hate him so I could pretend that was all I felt. It was a losing battle. I wasn't going to forgive him for what he'd done or excuse his refusal to help me. But I would've been lying to myself if I'd said being around him again didn't stir some-thing in me.

If he had been totally different from when we were younger, I could have pictured him as someone else. Not the same boy I loved once. Not the boy I wanted to spend every waking minute with. But the longer I spent around him, the more obvious it was that he hadn't changed much at all. He was still sweet, still concerned for me before himself. He still understood me better that I wanted to admit. It was his circumstances that had changed. Some small, stupid part of me thought how nice it might be if he could go with me when I left. But it was clear how dedicated he was to his family, however misguided that dedication might be. And if he couldn't walk away from them, there was no way I could be with him. I told myself that over and over, trying to forget that I wanted it, trying to ignore the sheets smelling like him.

9

ROGER

I flinched at the sound of her shoe hitting the door behind me. Nothing about that "conversation" was what I expected it to be. The sex was incredible, better than it ever was in the past. She was always so insistent on condoms when we were younger—so yeah, it felt different. But the way we'd talked afterward was just like I remembered. Her, cozied up to my side, us talking through a fight we'd had earlier, me explaining myself and her understanding.

Then I fucked it all up by bringing up Rena, and Jill wouldn't let go of the subject. It was easy for her to sit there and judge my feelings about my dad getting remarried; she still had both of her parents. But I had gotten too hung up on the thought and panicked so much that I had to leave before we got any more into the subject of my mom. That was the last thing I wanted to talk to Jill about. I wondered if this time she was sure about hating me, or if she might let me explain myself again later. For the night, I was definitely done talking.

With too much on my mind to go to bed, I wandered down the hall and outside to the pool, planning on walking a couple laps around it until I was too tired to keep thinking. My plans changed when I found Royce there, sitting at one of the deck chairs with a copita glass in one hand and a bottle of Dad's Yamazaki 18 on the table next to him. I didn't know what he was doing up that late, but he didn't drink often; he even had water at dinner when everyone else was drinking wine.

"Hey," I said as I walked up, and he nodded at me. "Mind if I join you?" He shrugged. After grabbing a tumbler from the bar, I came and took a seat next to him. "Does Dad know you took this?" Our dad wasn't even much of a drinker himself, but he was still stingy about anything that belonged to him.

"Probably not. But he was the one so insistent on me being here, so he can deal with it." We both took a drink, and I shuddered from how strong the whiskey was. Expensive as hell, but it was still a lot to handle. Royce didn't speak right away, so I tried again.

"How's Whitney doing?"

"She's fine. Resilient. She always has been. Happy to see you. Happy to see Myles. Misses her mom." He took another drink. "Can't really blame her for that."

"Do *you* miss her mom?" I tried to be casual sneaking a look at him. For the first time since he'd arrived, he smiled genuinely, just a little.

"Yeah. Some. It's complicated. You know that's why I left for Bristol, right?"

"Because of Margot?" No, I definitely didn't know that.

"Sort of." He took a deep breath and leaned back in his chair, staring up at the starless sky. "We split up because she was worried about this"— he gestured at the house — "Being bad for Whitney. And I agreed with her. I always agreed with her on that, but it took her leaving for me to understand how much she meant it. I left for myself, but I also left for them. To let Whitney grow up somewhere safer. And... Maybe to show Margot she could trust me to put Whits first. That I was done with all this and done with my father." His smile turned bitter as he swirled the whiskey in his glass. "And yet. Here I am again."

Shit. I had known when he'd left that it was for Whitney's sake, but I didn't realize his feelings for Margot were tied up in it too. I'd always thought they'd mutually agreed that it wasn't working between them. This was all news to me.

"You were trying to get her to take you back?" I asked, and he nodded slowly.

"And I think, for a while, it was working. She was willing to see me more often and talking to me more. I think she was *maybe* starting to trust me again. But this time, she's probably decided I don't get another chance." After draining the last swig from his glass, he poured in another healthy portion. "She fought me tooth and nail against bringing Whitney back here. And I had to explain that if I didn't, they would've both been..." He hunched forward over his lap, dropping his head and taking another slow, deep breath.

"I'm... uh..." What the hell was I supposed to say? He was basically explaining how our dad had ruined his entire fucking life by insisting he come back "home." And all the time he was gone, I had ignorantly been pissed at *him*.

"Don't." Putting his glass back on the table without taking a drink, he told me, "It's not your fault. Besides, he can't control me forever. I'm just counting the days." I wanted to ask "until what," but I had a feeling I knew already. Sitting back in his chair again, my brother threw me a look over his glasses. "Myles told me it's Jill in there. The grocery store girl. What are the odds, huh?"

"Slim to none, but here we are." Thinking about her and whatever the hell was going on between us, the way she'd just torn me down without hesitation, I took another drink.

"Is she talking to you? Myles said she was beyond pissed when you brought her back."

Again, his big brother influence was making me want to tell him everything, but I resisted. I'd told him all those years ago when Jill and I first slept together, and despite trying to tell me how stupid and dangerous it was, he couldn't help grinning and congratulating me afterward. This time, though, I was sure he'd think what I'd just done was a little *too* stupid. So I gave him a copy of his own dry smile and shrug.

"It's complicated."

He snorted a laugh. "Yeah, I bet." After a second, he got up from his seat and grabbed his glass to empty it into the grass. For good measure, he took the bottle to the end of the pool and, after wavering a moment, he chucked it as far as he could. We didn't see or hear when it landed, but the house was on a steep hill, so it was definitely long gone.

"Feeling better?" I asked when he came back.

"Look, the only thing that son of a bitch cares about is money. If that's how I have to get back at him, by God, I'm going to do it." He swayed a little on his feet after that passionate declaration, then steadied himself. He rubbed his temples. "I'm going to bed. Don't stay up too late." He smirked and ruffled my hair as he walked past.

"Fuck you, I'm a grown man," I called back at him.

"Whatever you say, kiddo."

I shook my head as I settled back in my chair, but my smile faded pretty quickly once he was gone. Sure, it was nice having him back, having someone around I could actually trust and talk to. Nicer than I expected. But if he was as unhappy as he seemed, if he and Whitney would be better off elsewhere, it seemed unfair and wrong to force them to stay.

THE NEXT MORNING, I slept in. Even when I woke up, I stayed in bed, thinking about the conversation—the *actual* conversation—I'd had with Jill. When I'd said I wanted to help her, I meant every word. I just had no idea where to start. The easiest thing would be if Fred would just pay up ASAP and I could let her go before she was there long enough to start really hating me. But then, that was part of what she'd laid into me for: doing the easy thing instead of the right thing, the thing I actually wanted.

As shitty as it made me feel, I forced myself to consider what she said. After the talk I'd had with Royce, it was getting easier and easier to think that maybe I was only there because it was easy, because I knew my dad would make my life a living hell if I tried to leave. Was avoiding that worth spending my life doing whatever he told me instead of pursuing my own ambitions? That was a tough decision to justify.

So what could I do for Jill short of just letting her go? How could I at least make this easier for her? I thought about her sitting down there in that tiny room, alone with nothing to occupy her, and I figured that was a good place to start. Maybe we could put her in a better guest room. Or even better, a different house altogether. We had a few spares around the city. If I could convince my dad to let me move her into one of them and stay to "keep an eye on her," it would give us some time alone. Together. And maybe it would be enough to convince her I was trying.

Around noon, while I was putting together my argument for why Jill needed to be moved, there was a knock at my bedroom door.

"Yeah?"

The door opened and Myles stuck his head in, looking like a kicked puppy. "Dad wants to talk to you," he said. My first fear was that he knew I'd slept with Jill the night before. But judging by how completely deflated Myles looked as he left, I figured he'd just come out of the same talk. And it wasn't a good one. Convincing him about this plan of mine was only going to be harder if he was already in a shitty mood, but I had to try. I got up and dressed, hoping I'd be able to talk to him calmly despite my feelings about Jill and my anger over what he'd done to Royce.

When I got to his office and knocked, he called, "Come in, Roger." He was seated as his desk, same as ever, eyes locked on his laptop screen with the same unimpressed look he wore 95% of the time. Even once I was standing in front of the desk, he made me wait a few seconds in tense silence before letting out a sigh and looking up from his laptop. "We need to get that girl out of the house."

I was all ready to start defending myself against whatever accusations he had lined up, but that threw me off. "What?"

He turned the laptop toward me, displaying a Twitter feed full of the hashtag #MorettiMob. Looking closer, I saw that most of the tweets were related to Jill's kidnapping—a lot of them including the video we'd watched last night—

but plenty of others were pointing out other crimes our family had committed over the years.

"One viral video of a white woman being harassed is all it takes to destroy a family's reputation, apparently," Dad said, leaning forward against his desk with his hands folded in front of him. "Now all sorts of conspiracy theorists and people who've been on the wrong end of our business in the past are coming out of the woodwork saying they'll testify against us. It's bad enough that some of my other network contacts are beginning to question me." His voice was low and hard with a kind of quiet anger I'd only seen on him a few times before. It never ended well. "How much money do you imagine it's going to take to smooth all of this over? How much do you think it'll cost to prove we can be trusted?"

"I..."

"It'll be more than the quarter million Fred Johnson owes me, I can promise you that. I sent you and Myles out to do a simple collection job, and you end up costing me time and money instead. And now we need the girl out of the house in case we get *searched* like some petty fucking criminals. I just wish I had the words to express how utterly disappointed in the two of you I am."

"It wasn't my—"

"Save it," he said, holding up a hand to stop me. "Myles told me what happened. And even though it was his stupidity that started this mess, you could have stepped in at any time to stop it. If you had bothered trying, I'm sure he would've listened to you. But you preferred to stay out of it and let him do the talking so you wouldn't have to get your hands dirty."

"You were the one who told me take him!" My hands clenched into fists at my side while I fought to control my temper. "Because you thought it would be 'entertaining'!

You fucking know what he's like just as well as I do, and you still sent him!"

"I assumed you would be able to control him." Dad didn't get up or raise his voice, but his tone was razor-sharp. "But you're right. I should have known I couldn't trust either of you with this. I should have waited until Royce got back." Hearing that just spiked my resentment toward him even higher.

"Why the hell did you make him come back in the first place?" I demanded, gesturing toward the door. "You know he's miserable. You know he doesn't want to be part of this anymore. And you know he doesn't want Whitney involved in any of it. Why are you forcing them to stay?"

"This is why, Roger." He indicated the laptop screen, where the tweets were steadily multiplying. "Because when I trust you or Myles with anything, this is what happens. Royce is smart. He may not like doing what we do, but he's good at it. That's more than I can say for Myles's overenthusiastic approach or your apathy. Royce is the only one of Latasha's children who's worth anything."

That last statement sucked the air out of my lungs. It wasn't the first time he'd told me I was worthless. It wasn't the first time he'd said I would never be as successful as Royce. But he had *never* brought our mom into it before. What was he trying to say? That Myles and I were defective? Because of her? No matter how I tried to frame it in my mind, it was an insult to her, and I wouldn't stand for it.

"You... how fucking dare you?" I snarled, leaning forward over the desk, barely holding myself back from hitting him, only because I knew what a mistake it would be. "You have no right—"

"If anyone in this house has the right, it's me." He finally got to his feet like he was challenging me to make a move, and even though I had a couple inches on him in height, it still somehow felt like he was bearing down on me. "You need to remember that the reason you're able to bitch at me over anything say is because I *allow* it. Remember that everything you have, everything you've ever had, has come from the business you're so reluctant to take part in. *My* work. I have every right, including the right to tell you when you're being a spoiled, ungrateful little shit."

My hands itched to swing at him and end this argument more decisively, but I realized I was starting to see red again and didn't want to give in to it. Instead of answering, I turned on my heel to march out of the office.

"Take the girl elsewhere, Roger," he called after me. I didn't answer, but I was definitely planning to get her the hell out of that house.

I headed for Royce's room and knocked on his door, impatiently tapping my foot until he answered. Looking at him, I wouldn't have guessed he'd had a quarter bottle of Japanese whiskey the night before. "What's up?" he asked.

"I need your help with something."

"You're going to have to be more specific than that."

"I'm trying to get Jill out of here."

He crossed his arms and leaned against the doorway, looking almost proud of me. "Really? And just ignore the boss's orders?"

"Oh. I just meant take her somewhere else," I muttered. I couldn't look at his face knowing it would show his disappointment. "She's in one of those shitty little bedrooms down the east hall. If she's going to be here, she might as well have some better digs."

"Such as...?"

"We have other places. You know more of them than I do."

"Hm." He thought about it for a second. "Would a safe house work? We have a few of those, and they aren't used often—"

"That sounds perfect."

"—which means it's probably empty at the moment," he continued. "You'd have to go turn on the power and the water. Since she won't be here with access to the staff anymore, you'll need to stock the kitchen too. And I'm willing to bet she'd kill—figuratively I hope — for some clean clothes." He noticed the way I looked at him, like he was some kind of expert on women's needs, he laughed. "I was married for eight years, Roger. You learn a thing or two."

"Help me," I pled, but his smile faded.

"Are you sure you want the help of a blood traitor like me?" he asked flatly. "Who knows, you start associating with me and people might think you're going to desert too." Had somebody said that to him? I realized too late that Dad had probably had a chat with him that morning too. All the more reason to get away from this place.

"I don't give a shit about any of that. You left. You came back. You're here now, and that's what matters. Besides, it's not like Myles knows anything about women, so he'd be totally useless here," I added, trying to lighten the mood a little. "And hey, if you're not in the house, Dad can't order you around."

"I guess that's true." He still didn't seem convinced, so I conceded to trying the sincere approach instead.

"Look, Royce, cards on the table. I've really fucked things up with Jill, and this is not the first time it's happened," I admitted. "I still care about her. A lot. And she fucking hates me right now. I want to do whatever I can to fix things between us. If you help me, I feel like I have a way smaller chance of screwing it up."

"Can't argue with that logic." He stood up straight and agreed, "Fine, but Whitney's going with us. I'm not leaving her in this house by herself."

10

JILL

A woman I didn't recognize showed up to bring me food in the morning. For a brief second, I considered trying to overpower her and escape, but I quickly decided it wasn't worth it for a lot of reasons. For one, she herself hadn't done anything to me, and judging by the modest uniform-like clothes she was wearing, she was probably just a domestic servant. Because the Morettis were the type of people to have servants. "Staff" was the word they had always used in the past, but we all know what it was. Especially the staff themselves.

Besides, even if I could've gotten out, where would I have gone? They would've just caught me and brought me back. So instead, I waited until she was gone, then attacked the plate of bacon and eggs she'd brought with her. After all the energy I'd used the night before, I was ravenous. It was shocking that they were willing to feed me so well, but I figured that whatever I was eating was just left over from The Family's meals. That made it a little less appealing.

More time passed. Hours. More silence. Realizing I smelled like sweat and sex, I cautiously took a shower in the little 3' x 3' glass box in my bathroom. No soap, but at least the water was hot. Once again, I was reluctant to put on my old, stale clothes, but what choice did I have? Better that than getting caught naked—especially by someone who wasn't Roger.

Roger. I didn't even know if he was planning to come back. I'd said some pretty hurtful things the night before. He might just leave me to wallow in my boredom until I was begging for company. After another couple of hours sitting, thinking about the store, hoping Annette was picking up my slack and helping Dad with managing, I was getting close to that point. The same woman brought me a second meal, but she obviously wasn't much for conversation. She acted like she was afraid to speak to me.

Then finally the door opened again. But it wasn't who I expected.

"How's it going in here?" Myles asked, leaning against the dresser by the door. "Comfortable?"

"I'm peachy. Thanks for your concern."

He laughed at my answer, but I noticed that his leering looks from the day before were nowhere to be seen. "Come on, I know you've gotta be bored out of your mind," he said. "Talking to me must be better than just sitting here. Even a little?"

"Marginally, maybe."

"See, that's what I always liked about you." He drummed his fingers against the top of the dresser, cocking his head to one side and watching me thoughtfully. "You were always just a little bit of a bitch and you weren't even sorry for it."

"If that's your idea of a compliment, I think you need some more practice," I informed him.

"It's just the truth. There's no point in acting like I don't know you already. Like we don't know each other. I don't want to pretend you're a stranger. Everybody here knows who you are. Hell, even half the staff probably remember you. For the four years you and Roger were together, you were at our place *all* the time. That doesn't go away just because you're pissed at us."

"Not here."

"You know what I mean," he said with a roll of his eyes. "In our lives. You were like, a fixture. You were family, whether you want to admit it or not. But here you are acting like we're just some big bad mob entity you don't know anything about."

"That's exactly what you are. Whatever memories you have of me are ten years old, Myles. We *don't* know each other anymore. I'm not close to any of you like I was before, and I'm not interested in pretending to be." I was trying to shut the conversation down, to get him to get bored or accept that I wasn't receptive, but he had always been more persistent than that. The searching look on his face didn't change, and if what I'd said bothered him, he didn't show it.

"It's really funny: I was trying to tell Roger that yesterday. But now I'm not so sure. I don't think you've changed as much as you want to believe. I mean, you've obviously still got the hots for my brother. Since you're so uninterested in pretending, you've probably admitted that to yourself already, huh?"

How could he know that? Was he just bluffing, trying to get me to admit something? "You're assuming a lot. What would even give you that idea? I haven't seen *him* in ten years, either."

"Oh, you two didn't have a little chat last night?" he asked, raising an eyebrow at me. Heat and embarrassment flashed through my core, and I immediately looked down at my lap so he wouldn't see me blushing. "Yeah, that's what I thought. I mean, I didn't hear any specifics, but it sounded pretty, uh, intense."

"Shut up," I muttered, grasping tightly at the sheets beneath me.

"Hey, don't get mad at me. I'm just making observations. I was saying you weren't interested in him anymore, but you proved me wrong, like, immediately. What did he do to piss you off so much?"

I sat still for a second as I realized that Myles was talking about hearing my shouting, not whatever I'd said while I was in bed with Roger. That was at least a slight relief. "None of your business."

"Probably, but I'm still asking. It's always been a talent of his, I know. I remember when you two would fight, you know, way back when," he mused, eyes turning up toward the ceiling. "And you fought like, bad. Brutal. You never got that mad at anyone else. Not even me, and we both know I was a little shit back then." I hoped keeping my head down would hide my smile. He absolutely was a brat, with a bad habit of teasing Annette, but he wasn't a bad kid. At least, not back then. "So I feel like it must be something special about him. Like it was then, and it's the same now. Either you *really* hate him or you—"

He stopped when the door opened again, revealing the Moretti brother I had expected to visit me. Roger looked in confusion between the two of us, then turned a mistrustful glare on Myles. "What are you doing in here?"

"Catching up," Myles said with an easy smirk. "Why? What else would I be doing?" He pushed off from the dresser and, with a last nod at me, left the room.

"Sorry," Roger muttered, watching him go. "Was he bothering you?"

"No more than usual," I said without thinking. Damn it.

I needed to keep reminding myself that these people were *not* familiar anymore. They weren't the same ones I had such fond memories of from years ago.

"So yes?" Roger's crooked smile was way too familiar, only adding to my internal conflict. I now noticed he'd cleaned up since the day before: his hair was washed and swept back, his facial hair neatly trimmed, his clothes a little nicer. Surely all that wasn't to impress me. Well, maybe I was a little impressed whether he intended it or not. After the way I'd thrown myself at him last night, I couldn't pretend like I *wasn't* attracted to him.

"Ahem. Don't worry about it," I said, tearing my eyes away from him. "Did you bring me some news or...?"

"Some, yeah," he said with a subtler knowing smile. Had he noticed me checking him out? *Oh God, how embarrassing.* "The bad news is I still can't let you go." Before I could get angry and snap at him again, he hastily continued, "But the good news is I can get you out of *here.* Somewhere more comfortable. I mean, I know it's not exactly what you want, but I was hoping it would help a little."

I nodded slowly, firmly, trying not to show how eager I was to be out of that room. "It's definitely a start. Where are we going?"

"We have a safe house outside town. An hour or so from here. You would have the place to yourself, so at least you wouldn't be stuck in one room." Again, his eyes wandered away from mine, and he shrugged. "And who knows, maybe I could, uh. Visit. If you'd be okay with that." Seeing him get so bashful, I couldn't help smiling back.

"Well, we'll see about that part," I said coyly, taking a step closer. "So, when do we leave? Soon?"

"As soon as you're ready."

I gave him an unamused look and gestured to myself.

"This is all I brought, so it's not like I have packing to do." After I put my shoes on, he led me out to the garage again. Rather than one of the ridiculously fancy sports cars, he led me to a more modest four-door Cadillac. Not much less conspicuous, but a little. What I noticed more was the fact that we weren't alone.

Standing by the car was a man roughly Roger's height, similarly good-looking but in a more mature way. When he smiled at me, his green eyes showed it was genuine. "Hey Jill," Royce said with a nod. "Long time no see." I had to resist the urge to hug him. What was it about him that gave off that Trustworthy Older Brother vibe? The glasses, maybe.

"Uh, yeah, it's been a while," I agreed, returning his smile. "You know, you're honestly the first person here I've been happy to see."

"Ooh, ouch," he said, shooting Roger a teasing grin.

"Are you going with us? To make sure Roger doesn't try anything?" I looked over at Roger, who raised an eyebrow as if to say *that's not what you said last night*, and I was forced to turn away from him again.

"Something like that. He's only ever been to this safe house a time or two, so I'm driving. Lucky for you."

"All right, can we *go* already?" Roger groaned. But somehow, pestering him along with his brother made me feel a little more comfortable around them. Like we were kids again.

"Fine, don't throw a fit." Royce stepped into the center of the garage and called out, "Okay, Whits, olly olly oxen free."

At first I didn't know what he meant, but then a tiny voice behind me shouted, "Boo!" and I jumped, squealing in shock. Turning around to look for the culprit, I found a little girl covering her mouth with both hands, giggling in delight from scaring me. Her thick black hair was pulled into bunches on either side of her head, and she was dressed like she came from money.

"Hey, you're a jerk, you know that?" Roger said, scooping her up to hold her under one arm while she kept laughing and tried to wrestle away.

"I was only joking!" she pled through her laughter. "Lemme go!"

"Um, who...?" I started. I had a guess but didn't want to assume.

Roger sighed heavily. "This little brat is my niece, Whitney. She's going with us today, and she better behave, or else I'll have to teach her a lesson when we get back." He put her back down on her feet, and she immediately rounded on him with her tiny fists up.

"I'm not scared of you, old man! Don't make me use my judo moves on you." It sounded like she had some kind of accent, and I remembered Roger saying they'd lived in the UK. Before their father forced them to come back.

"You're letting this kid learn judo?" Roger asked, looking up at Royce incredulously. "You *want* her to knock me out or something?"

"Hey, *you* try telling her she can't do something once she's set on it." Royce was still standing at the car with the driver door open, waiting on us. "But you kids will have plenty of time to play later. We should get going." He nodded at me and Roger. Whitney went ahead of me and climbed into the backseat behind her dad, leaving me to scoot in beside her while Roger took the front. The first thing I did was check the clock on the dash. 4:49 pm.

"You sure you remember how to drive on the right side of the road?" Roger asked playfully as Royce pulled onto the highway.

"Please, I went back and forth for years. I think I got it."

"Ahem. Uh, hi there," I said, leaning forward to try to get Whitney's attention. She looked up at me with warm brown eyes that practically glowed in the midday sun, and a smile to match. "I'm Jill. It's nice to meet you."

"You too! Uncle Myles said you and Uncle Roger used to date," she said brightly.

"Ugh." Roger groaned and rubbed his temples. "Uncle Myles needs to learn to keep his damn mouth shut."

"What a miracle that would be," Royce muttered.

"Well. He was right," I agreed, still trying to keep the conversation lighthearted. Something about Whitney's presence had changed the air of this interaction. It almost felt like I wasn't a prisoner, like this trip could be something fun. She wasn't part of their horrible family business; she was just a little girl with a big personality. And it was nice to see that, at least among these three, the word "family" wasn't just a title or an obligation. It was a real, loving relationship. "I did date your Uncle Roger when we were younger."

"Why did you stop?" she asked, oblivious to the tension between us. Royce glanced at me, then her in the rearview mirror.

"Sweetie, that's not really our business—"

"No, it's okay!" I said, waving him off. "It's fine. We had to break up because my family moved away. We didn't see each other for years, and it's hard to stay together like that." Maybe it wasn't the whole truth, but she didn't need to know all the details.

"But now you're back together," she pointed out, absently swinging her legs in front of her. "And you both live here, right? So you can be together again."

I let out a dry laugh. *It must be nice to be so optimistic.* "It's a little more complicated than that, unfortunately."

Whitney nodded sagely. "Because he kidnapped you." Despite how serious the situation was, I had to turn away to hide an involuntary smile, and Roger's snort of laughter didn't help.

"Yeah. Because of that. I don't really like his job," I said, stealing a glance at him.

"That's how my mum is too."

"Whitney." There was a warning in Royce's tone, but he didn't look away from the road. His smile from earlier disappeared completely. His daughter looked at him sadly for a second, then folded her hands and dropped her eyes to her lap. After another moment passed in silence, Roger turned around in his seat to look at her.

"Hey, Whits, why don't you tell Jill about the time we got lost at the zoo looking for you?"

As quickly as it had disappeared, her smile came right back. She led into a lengthy and detailed account of a time that Roger and Myles took her to the San Diego Zoo for her birthday, because Royce had to work last-minute. She acted out every part of the story, from the animal noises to surprisingly accurate impressions of her uncles. Roger occasionally jumped in to defend himself or correct her. I even caught Royce smiling a time or two.

If I hadn't already known, I never would have guessed this was a family of criminals. How could Royce, the bespectacled dad ever blackmail anyone? How could Roger, who obviously loved his niece so much, threaten anyone's life? And how could sweet Whitney, who was so full of laughter that it was contagious, have grown up surrounded by killers? It was getting hard to reconcile the two sides—the family and the business—with one another.

When Whitney had exhausted her theatrics and gotten absorbed in a game on her cell phone, I noticed Roger and

Royce having a quiet conversation of their own. Hoping to learn something useful that Roger might not volunteer on his own, I turned to stare out the window and pretended not to eavesdrop.

"... Not even surprised at this point," Royce was saying bitterly. "I've heard him say worse about her. I honestly don't know why they were ever together."

"She deserved better."

Who were they talking about?

"And you know Myles is only the way he is because he's looking for an attaboy from Dad. He's seen you and me become disappointments and doesn't want to end up like us."

"Whatever. If he wants the job, I say let him have it," Roger muttered.

"That's a terrible idea."

"If it means you and I can get out of it? What the hell do I care that he'll run the place into the ground?" I stole a look at Roger, watching him cross his arms and lean back harder against his seat. I could hear the anger in his voice as he went on, "It's just that the more I think about it lately, the more I don't want to fucking be here either." Maybe he had taken my comments to heart. Part of me felt guilty for being so harsh, but maybe it was something he needed to hear.

"Really. Any particular reason for that?"

I made sure I was looking at the window, pretending I hadn't heard anything, in case Royce glanced in my direction. Roger was silent for a few seconds.

"Just thinking," he said finally.

When we arrived at the safe house, I realized I should have been spending less time romanticizing the family that was holding me prisoner and more time trying to see if there was anywhere I could run for help. From what I could tell, though, it was pretty much in the middle of nowhere, sitting on a mesa with no other houses around. The Morettis liked their lone-house-on-a-hill aesthetic, apparently.

It wasn't quite as extravagant as their mansion in town, but it was definitely a nice place, more homey than opulent. The wrap-around porch and wooden beams added to that effect, and it seemed like a great place to watch the sunset from. Roger took me inside while Royce and Whitney got out to stretch their legs.

"This is it," he said, gesturing up to the high ceiling of the living room. In the far left corner, there was a staircase. To our right, the room opened up to an impressive kitchen/dining room, which he led me into. "So, everything you need should be here. You know, food, toiletries—uh, I had to guess at your size, but there are spare clothes in the master bedroom." He gestured to a door just past the kitchen.

"Wait. You bought me new clothes?" I asked, narrowing my eyes at him.

"I mean. I figured if you were going to be here more than a day or two, you'd get tired of wearing the same thing. That seemed like part of the essentials." Chancing a look at my face, he winced slightly. "Is it a problem? It wasn't like I could pick some up from your place—"

"No, it's not that. I appreciate it. You're the one who stocked this place?"

"Yeah? Who else would have?"

"I don't know. One of your servants?"

He grimaced uncomfortably. "Staff," he corrected. "I guess I could've asked them, but I felt like it was something for me to do. I'm the one who dragged you here. I'm the one who wants you to be comfortable. I should be the one doing the work to make it happen." I stepped close to him and stood up on my toes to kiss him. It was soft at first but quickly got hotter and deeper, and he pushed his hands through my hair to encourage me. When I let him go, he took just a second to catch his breath and let out a brief laugh.

"You know, your moods are hard to predict," he said. "I can never tell if you're going to kiss me or call me an asshole."

"Right now, I'm thinking of doing more than kissing you," I told him honestly. Grinning devilishly, he started to pull me into his arms, but practically on cue, the car horn honked from outside. Right. I had almost forgotten Royce and Whitney were there, probably waiting on him. This was just supposed to be a drop-off. With a sigh, I stepped away from him. "I guess you should get going."

"I'll come back," he assured me. "I probably can't get away tonight without anyone getting suspicious, but tomorrow...?" He made it sound like a question, like he wouldn't come back without my permission. Whether it was true or not, I appreciated the effort.

"I guess I'll see you then." Wanting to keep my eyes on him as long as possible, I walked with him back to the front door.

"So. I do have to lock the doors," he said, although he at least sounded sorry about it. "And it's a safe house, meaning nothing gets in or out without clearance. So there's no point trying to bust the windows or anything; you'll just set off the alarm and someone will come out to check on you."

"Don't worry, Roger. I'll be a good girl and stay right here until you get back." My voice and smile were so falsely sweet they made my bitterness clear.

"I'm sorry," he said, avoiding my eyes. "But at least you have a little more freedom here."

"Freedom," I scoffed. "Right." Probably aware that he could only apologize so much and that his apologies wouldn't actually change anything, he leaned down and kissed my cheek again.

"Seriously, that bedroom. Make sure you check it out." With a last meaningful look, he stepped outside and pulled the door closed behind him. I heard it lock not once but twice. Peering through the blinds, I watched him get into the car and kept watching until it disappeared down the winding road, out of view.

Then I was alone. Again. Even though I'd argued with him, Roger was right: this was definitely an improvement on my first room. I took a few minutes to wander the house and get acquainted with the layout. It wasn't a huge place. Aside from the living room and kitchen, the only other room on the ground floor was the master bedroom Roger had mentioned. There was a sliding glass door that led to the porch outside, and I tried yanking on it in the vain hopes of escaping, but it wouldn't budge. The glass itself seemed extra thick. I wondered vaguely whether the Morettis had custom-ordered bulletproof glass patio doors. It was supposed to be a safe house, and it seemed like they had committed to it fully.

As promised, the closet and dresser were full, and I wondered how long he had spent shopping. Had he been setting this up all day? Then I nearly swooned when I saw the gorgeous master bathroom and, more importantly, the huge, luxurious bathtub. I started filling it right away, eager for the opportunity to wash my hair since I had skipped it the day before. In the meantime, I took a closer look at the clothes Roger had bought, hoping something would fit and I could get out of the ones I'd been wearing for over twenty-four hours.

There was a little of everything, sometimes the same item in two different sizes. Most of it was practical, but there were also a few things just a little too sexy for casual wear. Maybe I should've expected that. I searched out the most comfortable pajamas I could find—trying to ignore the steep price tag still attached—and went to take my bath. As expected, it was heavenly. Once I'd finished bathing, I was reluctant to leave the comfort of the hot water. But eventually, it started to get cold, so I was forced to get out. It was a little after 7 pm by then, but I dressed in my pajamas, anyway; it wasn't like I was going anywhere.

Surprisingly, the worst part of my captivity so far had been boredom. I was so used to working twelve hours or more a day that suddenly being deprived of that focus made me insanely restless. With a frustrated sigh, I threw myself down on the bed and heard something clatter against the wall and onto the floor. A distinct and recognizable clatter. Kneeling next to the bed and inspecting the floor, I found my hunch was right. A phone! I scrambled to grab it as if someone would take it from me any second.

I immediately tried dialing my dad's number, but there was just a busy signal. I got the same from calling Annette. And even 911 wouldn't work. "Damn it!" Surely it wasn't a coincidence that it was there. Roger must have left it there for me—but if it didn't work, what was the point? I tried looking through the menu for any information, but all I found was a single contact. *R.* Of course. When I tried calling him, I actually got a ring.

"Took you long enough," he answered almost immediately.

"Is this some kind of game?" I demanded. "Making me think you were trying to help, then taking it away?"

"What? I *am* trying to help. I thought you'd be glad to have someone to talk to."

"And that someone just happens to be you."

It seemed like the only real change that had happened that day was my going from a prisoner to a pet. Set up nice and comfortable so I'd stop complaining. Isolated so no one else could access me. Even though some part of my brain believed he didn't mean it that way, that he really was trying to help in the little ways he could, another cynical voice suggested this was all part of some darker grand plan.

He sighed on his end. "You're not obligated to talk to me if you don't want to. You can hang up whenever you want. Just don't smash the phone or anything. I want to be able to reach you if necessary. I need to know you're okay out there and nothing's happened to you." I felt a little guilty for accusing him.

"I do want to talk to you." Maybe he was right and my moods *were* hard to predict. But that was only because I never knew if I could really trust him. No matter how much I wanted to, there was this doubt that kept sneaking back into my mind and making me feel defensive. I needed to work on keeping it in check until he proved himself one way or the other. "Well, I'm glad I got to meet Whitney. She seems so sweet."

"Oh, don't let her fool you. She really is a brat," he chuckled. "But she's still a good kid. Better than we were at her age."

"When you say 'we,' who do you mean?"

"Me and my brothers. I don't know about you. What were you like when you were eight?"

"I was an angel, thank you very much," I said indignantly, climbing back up on the bed to lie on my back while I talked to him. "I was well-behaved and very mature for my age."

"Yeah, that sounds like you." I heard a door open and close from the other side of the line.

"Where are you?"

"My room. I figured it was better to have this conversation somewhere it won't be interrupted."

"Oh yeah? What are you expecting this conversation to be about?" I teased.

"I just meant the fact that I'm talking to you. My dad probably wouldn't be thrilled if he knew I gave you a phone. But hey, if you want to tell me what you're wearing…"

"Shut up," I laughed, trying to play the suggestion off as a joke. I'd hardly had much real sex in my life, much less phone sex. If I tried to just wing it right then, I was sure I'd embarrass myself.

"It's nice hearing you laugh," he said, catching me off-guard. When I didn't answer, he cleared his throat and went on, "Uh, sorry, is that weird? I just know you've been pissed the whole time since yesterday—not that you don't have a good reason! It's just nice to think of you smiling instead. I always liked making you smile. Shit, that makes it weirder, isn't it?"

"No, don't worry," I told him, shaking my head and hoping he could hear the smile in my voice. This man had no issues acting like a tough guy when it came to dangerous moments, but if he thought he'd upset me, dissolved into nervous rambling. How could I not find that endearing? "It's fine. I was actually thinking the same thing about you earlier. Seeing you and Royce together, it was a lot like back then. Before things got more complicated."

He told me some about what was going on at Moretti

Central, Myles was depressed because their dad laid into him earlier. And even though Deron kept trying to bring him back into the fold, Royce was still resisting as hard as ever. He was worried about his daughter being brought up in such a violent setting, especially when she already had a fighting streak in her. The whole time, all I could think was that the entire family would be better off with someone other than Deron running the show. When I found myself yawning and realized we'd been on the phone for two hours, I asked Roger when he was going to visit me the next day.

"Whenever you want," he said. "I can bring lunch or something, maybe around noon, and stay for a couple of hours. If you want."

"That sounds nice," I admitted. "It's a date." Again, he chuckled a little nervously.

"Yeah. Okay. I'll see you then."

"I'll be here."

After we hung up, I glanced out the window and realized how dark it had gotten. And blinds on the glass door were open. Suddenly nervous about being alone in this strange house, despite Roger's assurance it was secure, I went to close them. So much for being tired. Taking the blanket from the bed and the phone Roger had left me, I went into the living room and hoped the TV mounted above the fireplace worked. It only got a few channels, but all I needed was one. With the news on as background noise, I curled up on the couch and tilted my head back.

It's a date. Thinking back on my conversation with Annette, I laughed harder than was necessary. Was *this* what it took for me to get a date? Finding out my dad had been lying to us for years and then getting kidnapped? I laughed until there were tears in my eyes and I was exhausted, ready to fall asleep.

Then hearing my name on the news woke me right up again. I looked at the screen, thinking I must have misheard, but no, there was my name pasted under a video of my confrontation with Myles and Roger at the store. I had seen some people recording, but I'd figured it would just end up on Facebook as some housewife's scandal of the week. When the screen switched back to the newsroom, and I saw who was reporting, I scrambled to turn the TV up.

"The incident has sparked a flood of legal complaints against the Moretti family, from counts of money laundering to attempted murder." I recognized that voice. As they displayed a long list of tweets all marked #MorettiMob, Brooke, my friend Brooke delivered the story in her best, most professional reporter voice. She must have been the one to take the video to the media. My eyes went wide, first when I realized her involvement, then at the long, long list of people who had been hurt by the Morettis.

"And the search continues for Miss Johnson even now. Authorities have stated that a search of the Morettis' estate has not uncovered any evidence of my Miss Johnson's presence, though they have not yet been cleared of suspicion in her disappearance. More on this story as it develops."

She smiled as they went on to whatever subject they had lined up next, the weather, the stock market, whatever; I couldn't think about anything but what she said. First, why did it feel so weird to see Brooke reporting my situation? Maybe the story was just assigned to her. Maybe because she'd brought it in, she was the one who got to deliver it. And in that case, I probably should've been happy for her. I *was* happy for her, in a way. I'd never known her to hold back a story because of her own personal involvement, so maybe it shouldn't have surprised me.

And on a different note: did Roger know about all this?

About the news coverage and his family suddenly getting all this publicity? He must have. Why hadn't he told me about it? Why hadn't he mentioned that their house was being searched?

"Oh, God."

That must have been the reason he had moved me. Not because he wanted me to be more comfortable. Not because he was actually trying to help. Because it was convenient. His dad may have even ordered him to. And he had acted totally casual, like it was out of the goodness of his heart.

My first instinct was anger. I wanted to scream. I wanted to throw that phone across the room and hear it smash. I thought about calling him back and demanding answers. But I didn't. I forced myself to sit there and took a deep breath in. Breathed out. Then took another. Because another part of me really wanted to believe he was being sincere. When he told Royce he wanted to get away from this life, it sounded genuine. And every time we talked, he was obviously happy to see me. I couldn't believe that was all put on. I didn't want to.

We could talk about it when he came over. I did plan to ask him, to make sure he had an answer that would satisfy me. If he didn't, *then* I could get pissed and throw a fit. Until then, I was going to have faith that there was more going on than I could see. And hope it didn't completely backfire.

11

ROGER

If I had been around anyone else, I would've worried about getting caught grinning like an idiot. Since I was alone, I didn't bother hiding it. Even if the reason for moving Jill out of the house wasn't exactly what I had in mind, it seemed like the change of scenery had done a lot to improve her mood. Somehow, talking to her about all the bullshit that was going on in the house made it just a little easier to deal with.

Myles had been miserable ever since we'd come back from dropping Jill off at the safe house. Either he was pissed that he wasn't invited, or he was stewing over Dad's griping. I couldn't tell which, and he'd retreated to his room to pout about whatever it was, broadcasting the sounds of machine guns and sniper rifles through the hall even louder than usual. I thought about going to check on him, but frankly, I didn't feel like being around him when he was like that; it always led to him attacking anyone who got close, and I wasn't ready to subject myself to that so that he might let off some steam.

For some reason I didn't understand, Royce had gone

back to working for Dad, just like before he left. Even after everything we'd talking about, he was helping him make the calls and deals necessary to shut down all the talk about our family. If anyone wanted us to go out of business, I would've thought it was him. We hadn't gotten the chance to talk about his apparent change of heart yet. Even when I tried that night, he kept brushing me off, saying he was busy, that he needed to get this or that done first. Despite being irritated and wanted to demand an explanation, I remembered I had plans of my own for the next day. So I left both my brothers to their devices and went to bed.

~

I woke to the sound of my phone ringing and scrambled to answer it in case it was Jill. "Hello?"

"Hi," said an unfamiliar woman's voice. "Is this... am I speaking to Roger Moretti?"

"Uh, yeah, this is him," I said, scrubbing my face to try to wake up.

"Oh, thank God. My name is Brooke Rodham; I'm a friend of Jill's," she told me. Still half-asleep, I had to struggle for a second to make sense of the situation.

"Wait, you're Jill's friend?" I repeated dully. "How did you get my number?"

"That's not important. I wanted to ask if Jill is okay. Is she with you?"

"Right now? No. I mean, yes, she's okay, but no, she's not with me," I clarified. Blinking my eyes clear, I sat up in bed and shoved my hair out of my eyes. Whoever this "friend" of Jill's was, I needed to remember that she didn't know about our relationship, and for the sake of the family's image, she wasn't supposed to know that we were treating Jill well. Wasn't it supposed to be a secret that we had her at all?

"If she's not with you, where is she?" the woman asked, her voice spiking with panic. "How do you know she's okay?"

"I was with her yesterday. She's fine."

"So you're keeping her somewhere? God, we've just been so worried. I've been up all night with her sister, trying to find out anything about where she is or how she is—hearing that she's all right is such a relief," she gushed, not letting me get a word in edgewise. "Are you the one who's been, er, assigned to her? I mean, are you monitoring her? I was hoping it would be you."

"What? Why?" Also, what the hell did she mean by "assigned to her"? Was this woman one of those mafia conspiracy theorists Dad had mentioned?

"Well." Her voice dropped a little like this was a secret between the two of us. "Annette told me that you two used to see each other. You were high school sweethearts. So I thought that if anyone there would be inclined to treat her well, it would be you. At least, I hope that's the case. You don't have a grudge against her for leaving, do you? You're not mistreating her out of resentment, are you?"

"What the hell are you talking about?" Had Annette really told her the entire story? The longer I spoke to this woman, the more I got the feeling it was a mistake. "Look, whoever you are, I don't have time to sit here and play Twenty Questions. If you're actually Jill's friend, I'll let you know that she's fine. That's all you need to know."

I ended the call before she could go into another string of questions. I would have to remember to ask Jill about her. Something told me she wasn't being completely honest about their relationship.

When I went downstairs, Royce was still working, looking like he hadn't even stopped to sleep. By that point I was starting to get worried about him. At breakfast, I tried to ask Myles what he thought was going on, but he got surly as soon as Royce's name was mentioned.

"I don't know what the hell he's thinking," he grumbled, hunched over his plate and stabbing at his food with a fork. "How can I? He's the only one of us with a fucking brain, after all."

"You're still thinking about that bullshit Dad said?"

"Yeah, I guess it must be nice to have a convenient distraction waiting to suck your dick and take your mind off things," he muttered. I had to tamp down the anger that bristled at hearing him talk about Jill like that. We both knew that when he felt shitty about himself, his instinct was to make everyone else feel the same. He really was a lot more like our dad than anyone wanted to admit.

"So find something to do instead of just sitting here feeling sorry for yourself," I said, getting up from my chair. A harsh clang of metal on drywall told me Myles had thrown his fork across the room.

"You don't fucking get it!" he said, at a volume barely below shouting as he glared up at me. "You think I haven't tried finding something to do? You think I haven't tried helping fix this mess I started? Dad's not *letting* me. 'You've done enough,' he says. 'Just let Royce handle it.' He's already written me off as a fucking idiot and not of any use to him." He dropped his head into his hand, staring down at the table and shaking his head. "One stupid mistake, and he thinks I'm worthless."

I sometimes forgot how young Myles actually was. Maybe all of us did, him included. "Myles, listen—"

"Don't." He shoved to his feet and stalked past me, shaking his head. "Just. Don't bother."

Between his shitty self-esteem, Royce's obvious exhaustion, and my resentment, I wondered whether Dad even noticed that we were unhappy. Doubtful. He was probably in his office thinking about how smoothly things were running now that Royce was back. As if I needed any more of an excuse to get out of the house. If Dad wasn't accepting help from Myles, he probably wouldn't want it from me either. So I left to meet with Jill instead.

I thought about going by her family's store to see how things were going, if her sister and her dad were holding up okay. But being seen there was probably about the worst idea I could have. However they were doing, I just hoped Fred was taking this to heart and working on paying us back. And that my dad wouldn't charge extra for all our trouble.

After running through some Chinese takeout drive-thru —did Jill still like Chinese? I figured I'd find out—I headed to the safe house. It was pretty quiet from the outside, but when I got to the door, I could hear the TV. At least she'd found something to entertain her. Trying to downplay the whole "I literally hold the keys to your freedom" thing, I knocked and waited for her to let me in.

"It's twelve fourteen," she pointed out as she let me in. "You're late."

"Yeah, sorry. Forgot I had to pick up food."

While she was looking through the bags I'd set on the counter, I gave her a once-over. She was wearing some of the clothes I'd bought the day before, a pair of shorts and a thin t-shirt. And no bra again. She must have done that on purpose, right? Noticing the way my eyes kept coming back to her chest despite me trying to stop them, she laughed.

"You've obviously never gone bra shopping before," she said, crossing her arms. Well, yeah, when would I have? "The ones you bought are all padded or push-ups. Not really comfortable for sitting around the house. I washed mine, but it's still drying."

"Uh. Sorry. To be honest, I was trying to get that part done as fast as possible," I confessed, forcing my eyes down to the ground. Royce had made fun of me the entire time for being so "childish" about it, but there was a difference between going into one of those lingerie stores *with your wife* and going in to buy shit for a sort of ex-girlfriend.

"It's okay. You'll just have to deal with the consequences." She laughed again, and even though I knew she was laughing at me, I couldn't be mad. "These are fine, though." When I looked up to see what she meant, she had the waistband of her shorts pulled down a little on one side and it showed the thin strap of the black thong she was wearing. Fucking hell. I swallowed hard.

"Listen, if you want me to be able to focus on this conversation, you're gonna have to—" She ignored me and came closer to wrap her arms around my neck, pressing her tits against my chest and smiling like she knew exactly what she was doing. I had to fight to keep my hands off her so she couldn't accuse me of using her for sex again. Had she been thinking about me while I was gone? Again? I really liked that idea. "Jill..."

"I'm not really hungry at the moment," she said, just as casual as can be. "And I'm getting a little tired of Spanish soap operas. Now that you're here, I'm expecting you to entertain me." Without sparing any force, she dragged me down to meet her lips. And how was I supposed to keep fighting when she was being that insistent? I'd figured there was a 50/50 chance my visit would go this direction; if it was what she wanted, I'd gladly give it to her.

Bending down a little to get my arms around her waist, I picked her up and set her on the counter in front of me. That put her at just the right height for me to grind my hips into hers to show her how that pushy flirting was already effecting me. She managed to break away from my lips and let out a gasp and a moan, but my grip on her thighs held her still so she had to feel every bit of it.

"Mm, Roger?" she panted, leaning back on her hands and raising her hips to meet me. "Can I ask you something?"

"Right now, you can do pretty much anything you want." God, she was soft, and my body drew up memories of the other night. I wanted to explore that softness all over again.

"Why—ooh. Why didn't you tell me the house was getting searched?" she breathed.

I pressed my lips against her neck and ran my hand under her shirt before I realized exactly what she had said. Despite every instinct telling me not to, I pulled away a little to meet her eyes, and she was watching me critically. "What?"

"I was watching the news last night. Apparently people are looking for me. You never mentioned that yesterday when you were generously moving me to my fancy new cage." She glanced down at her breast where my hand was still resting, so I pulled away. Was this little seduction routine just a plan to get me to answer her? If so, she must really not trust me to tell the truth.

Taking a step back, trying to clear my head and calm my body down, I answered, "No, I didn't mention it. Because it's probably going to blow over soon."

"Blow over?" she repeated. "What does that mean?" I practically had whiplash from the quick change of subject, and I *really* didn't want to have this conversation with her. No matter how I spun it, she wasn't going to like where it went. But I wasn't about to lie to her either.

"It means my dad has friends in high places," I explained, sitting down on one of the stools at the island. "Higher than you might think. He's going to pay off or intimidate whoever he has to in order to make this go away."

"He can't pay all of them off. All those people coming out to talk about the things you—your family has done wrong. He can't shut them all up." A few years ago, I would've thought that too, but I'd seen it happen too many times.

"No, but he'll shut up the most important ones. Once the others realize nothing's going to come of it, they'll stop too." Again: not fair, not right, but it was what would happen, anyway. Jill frowned hard, turning her eyes down toward her lap. "I didn't tell you because I didn't want to get your hopes up."

"Yeah, I guess it's a lot easier to keep me under control if I'm hopeless," she said dryly.

I sighed in frustration, touching her arm to try to get her to look at me. "No, I just didn't want to tell you there might be a solution when I know he won't let it happen. I know you have a hard time believing it, but I'm on your side here, babe." When that word left my mouth, I flinched and dropped my eyes to the counter. I must've been getting too comfortable talking to her and arguing with her if that had come out by reflex. "... Sorry."

"I want to believe you," she said quietly. "I do. But you have to understand *why* that's hard, all things considered. All I know about the situation or anything that goes on outside of here is what I'm being told, usually by you. That's how I know about my dad's debt. That's how I know what's happening between your dad and Royce. And I don't have any way of knowing for sure whether you're being honest. It's a lot to take on faith."

"Yeah. I get it." We sat there together in silence for a few seconds, listening to the hushed Spanish dialogue from the TV. Eventually, Jill reached across the island toward the bags I'd brought in, so I handed her a box of fried rice and a fork. My lo mein was getting cold by the time I ate it, but not enough to put me off. Instead of continuing our conversation, we took a time-out to eat. Just sitting together.

The whole time, I was trying to come up with some way to convince her she could trust me. *I* knew I was totally sincere. How could I get her any kind of concrete proof besides my word? This was obviously a huge conflict for her, but short of swearing off my entire family, what could I do to fix that? And why did I want to so bad? Why were her comfort and peace of mind so important to me?

She caught me staring and smiled sheepishly, hopping down from the counter. "Come here." Grabbing my hand, she pulled me up from my seat and over to the couch to sit next to her. And she curled her legs up on the cushion beside her, getting comfortable against my side. "Maybe I can find us something better to watch." While she flipped through channels, I slid my hand up the back of her neck and into her wavy brown hair, catching the little smile that started on her lips. This was such a weird, unpredictable on-again, off-again thing happening between us, but I was still glad it was happening. I wanted it to keep happening.

After finding some spy movie and deciding it was as good a choice as any other, she put the remote down and leaned closer against me. The longer my fingers slid through her hair, rubbing against her scalp, the more she relaxed, her eyes falling shut, her head tilting forward. A time or two, she even let out a soft sigh or a moan. By the time I turned her toward me, she was already raising her head and letting her lips part to meet mine.

My tongue slid along her lower lip, slow, like she liked, then inside. She leaned forward to kiss me back, and while my tongue was in her mouth, she started sucking on it gently. That was something she'd never done before. For about the first half a second, it threw me off, but it quickly became insanely hot, and all I could think about was putting my cock in her mouth. She must have been thinking along the same lines, because she trailed her hand down the buttons on my shirt to my belt and started to unfasten it.

"Fuck," I muttered, pulling away from her to catch my breath, and she laughed at me again. Not teasing or ridiculing, just playful. I kept one hand in her hair while she was running her tongue up my neck and getting my pants undone. When she reached inside and found me already hard, she moaned deeply again.

"Is this okay?" she asked breathlessly, kneeling on the couch next to me and looking up into my eyes.

"I told you, whatever you want." As if I could complain about this! Pulling my pants and boxers down a little so they were out of her way, Jill leaned down and slid her tongue wetly up the length of my dick. My hand clenched in her hair by accident, and she gasped. "Sorry! Shit."

"Don't worry," she laughed, staying focused on what she was doing. "I'm fine." Again her tongue slid up and down me, and again, then her hand wrapped around and stroked me, all that wet friction that made me shudder and groan. After a second, she stopped and sighed. "This is hard to do from here." She crawled to the floor to kneel between my legs, pushing my knees apart to make room for her.

Brushing her hair back over her shoulder, she bent down again and put her lips around my cock.

"Fuck yeah," I muttered, still holding her hair tight but trying hard not to push her. How was she still so good at this? How did she still know exactly what I liked? Her head dropped down a little more, and she whined with effort before pulling back to catch her breath.

"Mm. It's been a while," she said, like she was embarrassed, like she wasn't fucking amazing. "Am I still doing okay?" She met my eyes again and bit her lip.

"Babe, you're incredible," I told her plainly, and she managed a smile past her blushing.

"Good." She put her head down and took me back in, sliding down, then back up, then down again, taking me deeper every time. She didn't seem bothered by me calling her that. It almost seemed like she even liked it. I'd have to keep that in mind. Assuming I could still think after she was done with me. The way her mouth moved, her tongue, the whimpers and moans she let out while she sucked me off— that would've been enough to drive any man crazy.

"God, that's so fucking good." Now and then, she'd have to take a break to breathe, but her hand picked up where her mouth left off. Besides, seeing her face flushed, her lips pink and shining wet, I didn't mind waiting. I got her to look at me once with her mouth still full, but she quickly got embarrassed and turned her eyes back downward, speeding up her bobbing to distract me. "Shit. Mm, I'm getting... close, babe. Don't stop."

She moaned around me and kept going, digging her nails into my leg. When the heat got too intense, and I finally came, I couldn't keep my hips from bucking up into her mouth, groaning out loud into the thick air while cool pleasure rushed through me. As I was struggling to calm down, I glanced down at Jill to see her swallow, still blushing hard. With shaky hands, she reached for a cup of water that was sitting on the coffee table and took a long drink. Once she'd set it down, and I was sure she wouldn't spill it, I grabbed her without a word and dragged her into my lap for another rough kiss. She practically melted against me, but I could tell from her weak participation that her mouth was exhausted.

"You okay?" I asked, running a hand up and down her spine while she rested her head on my shoulder. "That was... unbelievable." She giggled absently.

"Yeah. I'm good. But..." She trailed off and ground her hips against my thigh, breathing another soft moan in my ear. I was already working at getting her shorts off, pushing her down onto her back. Despite being a little shy about opening her legs, she did, watching me expectantly. I caught her lips again and leaned over her on one hand, sliding the other one between her legs. Again, she got her arms around my neck and refused to let me break away from her for even a second.

When my fingertips were soaked with her wetness, she hummed eagerly against my lips. When I touched her clit, she gasped but held onto me tighter. When my fingers pressed inside, she jerked away from me just long enough to catch a breath, then kissed me again. Something about her holding onto me like that, making a point of keeping me so close, got to me more than I'd expected. Hoping to pay back all the good she did me, I curled my fingers inside her, rubbing my thumb in circles over her clit while she squirmed and arched and whined.

She had to break our kiss when she started getting close, but instead she used her mouth to tell me how good I was and how much she wanted it. When she came, she let out a high-pitched cry, then devolved into a deep, grateful moaning, even smiling while her hips worked against my hand. And I got her to cum a second time before she weakly tapped on my shoulder, laughing breathlessly, eyes bleary. It seemed like she was having a hard time talking there for a minute, just grasping weakly at my shirt and trying to stay as close to me as possible.

"That good, huh?" I teased, and she mumbled wordlessly at me. There wasn't a lot of room on the couch, even less than her bed back at the house. So I just reversed our positions, lying on my back with her resting on top of me. Eventually, she did find her voice, and she slowly pushed herself up to look at me.

"Can you stay this time?" she asked, running her thumb along my jawline.

"You mean stay the night?"

She frowned at the doubt in my tone. "I guess that's a no."

"I mean, I can stay for now," I said quickly. "It's still early. But my dad won't be distracted forever, and if I just disappear, he'll start to notice something's up."

"And then what?" It wasn't an accusation. For once, she didn't seem mad about the subject of my family and my responsibilities to them. "What would happen if he found out you were here with me?"

"I don't know for sure. But I wouldn't put it past him to try to keep me away from you. Say you're distracting me or something." Or maybe he wouldn't like it because it wasn't his idea. Maybe he wouldn't like it because it was making me happy, which could be a problem for him at some point. Plenty of reasons to keep it a secret.

"If he told you to stop seeing me, would you?"

"You say that like he'd give me a choice. If he wanted it to stop, he would stop it," I muttered without thinking about how final it sounded.

"Would you fight it, though?" She almost sounded hurt, like hopeless that I would bother going to that much effort for her. But I wasn't about to lie to her.

"Yes."

Jill glanced up at me, somewhere between surprised and doubtful. "Really?"

"Yes. Look, I know we got off on the wrong foot this time around, but I'm glad I'm getting to see you again. Even once all this is over, once your dad doesn't owe us anymore and you go home," I said, wishing my mouth weren't so dry, "I'd like it if I could still see you. Obviously I understand if you'd rather not—"

"I haven't decided yet. For the moment, I'm going to stick with a firm 'we'll see.' But just so we're clear," she said, leaning down to kiss me again, softly this time, "in spite of everything, I'm glad I got to see you again too."

12

JILL

Even though Roger tried to tell me I was fine without them, I still put my clothes back on before settling onto the couch with him again. We sat there the rest of the afternoon, trading family stories that had happened over the past ten years. I talked about my plans for the store and how my dad seemed to be losing his passion for the business. I talked about my worries for Annette's future, how no one really seemed to know what she was planning to do, her included. I thought about asking if he had the same worries over Myles, but I figured our older-sibling experiences probably weren't really comparable.

He mentioned being worried about both his brothers in different ways: Myles because he was so desperate for approval and depressed when he couldn't get it; Royce because he'd so suddenly and doggedly started working for their dad again without any indication of why. At least he had the option of talking to them. I was starting to realize that I had taken things like that, like the ability to call my sister up and ask how she was doing, for granted.

Once I was out of this mess, I wouldn't make that mistake again.

"Hey." He stopped at one point and squinted at the TV, then reached for the remote to turn it up. The news was on again—was it five o'clock already?—and there was Brooke, professional as ever, with her name printed at the bottom of the screen. The graphic in the corner still featured the #MorettiMob hashtag, so I figured she was the one reporting it at her station, exclusively.

"What's wrong?" I asked, glancing at Roger, who was still staring suspiciously at the TV. "Oh. This whole story must be bothering you. Have you been—"

"No, it's that woman," he said without taking his eyes off her. "That's Brooke Rodham?"

"Yeah. Do you know her?"

After another few seconds of watching and listening, he sat back against the couch. "She didn't sound like that on the phone."

"What? When did you talk to her on the phone?" Had he contacted her on purpose? Trying to suppress the story, maybe?

"She called me this morning," he explained. "I don't know how she got my cell number, but she did. She was all broken up and worried about you, told me she was a friend of yours and asked if you were okay. *Is* she your friend?"

"Yes! She wasn't making it up or anything." I wanted to laugh, but something about this little revelation was leaving a bad taste in my mouth. "We've known each other for a few years, actually, so of course she was worried about me. She probably used her networking connections to find out your number."

"Right." If my reassurance was making him feel any more confident in her sincerity, he didn't show it. "A fucking reporter. Of course. That's why she asked a million questions in a minute."

"Oh, yeah, she's like that. I don't think she even realizes that she does it; she just has this instinct to get as much information as physically possible in any conversation." It was something we'd talked about before, something she had said she would try to work on. But when her job required her to be that way, it was a tough habit to break.

"I was able to conduct a brief phone interview with Roger Moretti this morning," Brooke was saying. "He had this to say."

There was an audio clip of an exchange between the two of them. She was right; it was very brief. Roger actually sounded like he'd just woken up. The conversation ended with him telling her firmly, "Look, she's fine. That's all you need to know" and hanging up.

The camera went back to Brooke. "As you heard, Mister Moretti confirmed that he does have Miss Johnson in custody, even if not at their home here in the city. Police and civilians alike are working tirelessly to find Miss Johnson before any further harm comes to her."

Roger's mouth had fallen open while he listened. "Holy shit," he said, scrubbing a hand over his face. "That fucking bitch!"

"Roger..." I protested weakly. Even if Brooke was my friend, which she had never mentioned in her report, I couldn't deny that she was being manipulative here.

"She recorded the conversation, babe! She never mentioned she was a reporter or that anything I was saying would be on record. And she wanted to play up that whole 'oh I'm her friend and I'm worried about her' angle. Did she look worried to you?" he demanded, gesturing to the screen.

"Well, when she's on camera, she has to look composed."

I only argued because I wanted to give Brooke the benefit of the doubt. It definitely did look a lot like she was playing up *my* story for her own sake. But maybe it was just a "right place, right time" sort of thing. "I don't know what she's thinking, okay? Whatever it is, I'm sure her intentions are good."

"Sure." Roger was obviously unconvinced, but I didn't know how to keep arguing with him, especially when I wasn't really confident in my stance.

When he had to leave soon after, I was genuinely sad to see him go, and not just because I was going to be bored out of my mind without him there, which I was. In spite of myself, I was enjoying spending time with him. Once he was gone, I thought more about our earlier conversation. Whether he would really be willing to go against his dad's plans and directions in order to be with me. It was a nice thought, but there were plenty of obstacles to it working out long-term. Oddly enough, I wanted to make the most of this time when I was forced/allowed to be around him without having to make the decision myself.

Well, I did say I wanted a vacation. And I never would've taken it willingly.

Roger called me again that night and promised he would come back the next day, the same time. Instead of making a passive-aggressive remark about how I couldn't leave, I told him honestly that I was looking forward to it.

∾

I ALMOST ASKED Roger to bring Royce and Whitney with him. Even Myles could come, if he would behave himself. I was just so tired of being alone! Before all this, my daily routine had involved interacting with hundreds of people over the course of twelve hours. Being there by myself was giving me way too much time to think. There was even a period where I started worrying that my rediscovered feelings for Roger were just a bizarre form of Stockholm Syndrome. That was the point when I tried working out for a few hours. Desperate, I called Roger and asked him to bring me books when he came to visit. *Anything* that would occupy my mind.

He showed up with a bag of Mexican food in one hand and a bag of books and magazines in the other. "I didn't know what you'd want to read, so I got a little of everything," he said with a shrug as I looked through the selection. Mystery novels, romance novels, fashion magazines, Sarah Silverman's autobiography. Surely there was something there that would entertain me.

"This is great. Thank you." I stood up on my toes to kiss his cheek, and he smiled slightly, but he didn't seem as happy as he usually was to be around me. "Is something wrong?"

"I don't know. Things aren't great back at the house." He started taking out Styrofoam containers of food: rice and beans, enchiladas, all of which smelled amazing. "I'm really getting worried about Royce. I finally got him to talk to me last night. He told me the reason he's been working so hard, trying to cover up for what me and Myles did, trying to keep people from questioning the family, is because he's worried about Whitney."

He sat down at one of the island stools and rested his arms on the counter in front of him. "Dad told him that if anything were to happen, if we actually got taken in—which we won't, obviously, because our name is too big—Royce would get dragged down with the rest of us." Roger hesitated, seeming uncomfortable, unsure of whether he should keep talking. "He's done some things, Jill. Working for our dad, you end up getting your hands dirty pretty quick. Like that's how you prove your loyalty. So if all that caught up with him, he'd end up getting put away for... a while."

"And then he wouldn't be able to see Whitney," I concluded. "Her mom is still around, isn't she? So it's not like Whitney would be on her own." Even while I was saying it, I knew it wouldn't be much of a comfort to Royce.

"Yeah, but she's everything to him. If Margot got full custody, and he never saw her again, I don't know if he'd be able to handle it." Roger was staring down at his hands, but his eyes were out of focus. I had seen him worried before, of course, but never this much. Then his face darkened and his hands clenched into fists. "And he wouldn't have to fucking deal with any of this if our dad would've just let him go."

"Your father is a monster," I said quietly. "Using Royce's daughter against him like that. It's disgusting." He didn't answer. Trying to offer whatever kind of solace I could, I took a step closer and laid my hand on his arm. After a second, the tension melted out of his shoulders. He took my hand in his and kissed my fingers.

"I'm sorry. I shouldn't be putting all this on you. It's not your fault. Not your job to fix any of it."

"Why don't you just leave, Roger?" I blurted without meaning to. He blinked in surprise, but his eyes quickly glazed over like this was an argument he didn't want to have.

"I've been thinking about it," he admitted. "Especially lately, seeing Royce deal with all this and. Seeing you again. But it's more complicated than just packing up and walking away. My dad's biggest concern is controlling everything and everyone around him. That goes double for his own kids. That's why he can't let us do anything he wouldn't do."

"What about Rena? She must see what's going on, and

I'm sure she knows it's wrong. Couldn't she try to talk some sense into him? If there's anyone he'd listen to, surely it's her." Even as I was saying it, I knew it wasn't likely. Their relationship dynamic just didn't work that way.

"She's not really a confrontational person," he said, shaking his head. "And definitely not one to disagree with my dad. I don't think she's even aware of half the shit he does. If my mom was still around, she would be fighting him every step of the way. Royce is the one who's the most like her, but even he can't stand up to Dad in a way that will actually make him listen."

Another big difference between Roger's family and mine. Annette and I had always been close, and our relationship with our parents was just as good. Since the move to San Diego, our parents hardly fought anymore, either. I didn't really know the feeling of needing to "stand up to" your own father.

"If you did try to leave," I ventured carefully, "what could he do to bring you back? You said Royce had an ex-wife, and obviously there's Whitney. That's how your dad manipulated him into coming back here. But you don't have anything like that. So what could he do to you?"

"Trying to leave on my own would mean abandoning Royce and Myles here," Roger pointed out. "Just let them deal with Dad's abusive bullshit while I run off for my own sake? I can't do that to them. I'd feel like a traitor."

Was he saying that it wasn't his dad keeping him there but some insistence on sharing in his brothers' pain? "So it's better if you all suffer together?"

To my surprise, he turned his hard frown on me like I had said something insulting. "Yes. And look for a way to stop it together. I know you and I have different ways of looking at family and the responsibilities we have to them, but my brothers and my niece aren't negotiable. I can't do that every-man-for-himself shit when I could've stayed and helped them. I won't. Even if that means suffering with them until we can find a way out of it."

Even if it wasn't exactly the answer I wanted to hear, seeing his conviction definitely made me feel something. "Sorry. I wasn't thinking about it like that," I admitted. "I just feel like if your dad is *that* committed to keeping you all in line, if you can't leave without being dragged back and you think there's no one who can convince him he's in the wrong —what are you supposed to do?"

He pushed a hand through his hair and dropped his head back. "I'll let you know when I figure it out. Look, can we talk about something else? I only get to see you for a few hours, and that's too important to let him ruin it."

"Of course." I leaned down and kiss him, slowly. The way he talked sometimes and the value he put on spending time with me made my chest warm and fluttery in a way I'd never felt with anyone else. That was how he'd always looked at me. Like I was making his life better just by being in it.

Over lunch, we talked about my little apartment and what it was like living there. Roger asked whether it was anything like living there at the safe house, and I had to detail the long list of reasons it was *not*. The longer we talked, the more comfortable I felt, and the more I liked the idea of keeping it up once I was no longer a hostage. My dad would hate the idea, I was sure, but when he had so much explaining of his own to do, I wasn't sure that mattered to me. God, I was really letting myself get in too deep, and I was starting to question whether that was really such a problem.

13

ROGER

After lunch with Jill, I got back to the house to find Whitney sitting on the steps outside. She had a handful of gravel from the driveway and was throwing the tiny rocks one by one out into the grass, her face drawn into a frown between sadness and frustration.

"Hey, Whits," I said as I walked in her direction. She didn't look up. "What're you doing out here?"

"Sitting." Even though the answer was a playful one, it didn't come through in her voice. I sat down beside her and nudged her shoulder.

"Yeah, I can see that, smart mouth. Why are you sitting out here in the heat instead of inside? Is something wrong?"

"I dunno. I just kind of feel like nobody here likes me."

"What? Why would you think that?" Was someone in the house rude to her? Some of the staff? I was already gearing up to fire someone over the hurt in her voice. "Who doesn't like you?"

"Anybody. Papa"—that was what she called our dad—"Keeps looking at me weird. I don't know if he's mad at me or something, but he doesn't say anything. He just looks at me. And it makes me feel like I did something bad, but I don't know what."

"Yeah. He makes a lot of people feel like that. It doesn't mean he doesn't like you. His face is just permanently grouchy." She smiled at that, but only slightly. "Who else?"

"None of the house staff wants to talk to me. It's like they're scared of me."

"Probably because you keep threatening people with judo attacks."

She shook her head, messy hair fluffing out around her. "No, I mean for real. Like they think they'll get in trouble for talking to me or something. Uncle Myles doesn't want to be around me either. When I try to talk to him, he just says 'hey' and then walks off. Sometimes he looks at me like Papa does, and then I feel like they're both mad at me for the same thing but I don't know what it is." Tears were starting to pinch her voice, forcing her to stop every few seconds to take a breath. "And... and Dad is too busy to talk to me. Like when we... lived here before. And I hate it...!"

"Hey, hey, come here." I moved closer on the step and put my arm around her shoulders, letting her cry into my chest. Whitney wasn't the kind of kid who cried a lot. Even when she got physically hurt, she barely even sniffled. I'd always thought that meant she was tough, but maybe it just wasn't that kind of pain that got her. "Your dad is not too busy for you. He's never too busy to care about you."

"But he can't talk to me," she managed, muffled with her face buried against my shirt. "I've... barely seen him since we got here."

"Well. It won't be like this forever. He has an important job to get done right now. But once that's over—"

"That's what he always says!" She sat back, scrubbing at her eyes with both hands to try to dry her tears. "He just has this one job. Then he'll be done. But then there's another job. And another. All he does is work when we're here." There wasn't really much I could say to argue with that. Since Royce was apparently the only one of us who was competent, Dad always had more work to dump on him. No wonder he wanted to leave so badly.

"I'm sorry, Whits," I muttered, running a hand over her hair. "It's not his fault. You know he'd spend all his time with you if he could." After another few sniffles, it seemed like she was done crying and back to being stone-faced. She pulled her knees up to her chest and wrapped her arms around them.

"I talked to Mum today."

That should've been a good thing, but judging by her tone, I figured otherwise. "Yeah? How did that go?"

"She's angry." Of course she was. "She tries to act like she isn't, but I can tell. She didn't even ask to talk to Dad. It seemed like they were getting on all right until we came back here. I just wish we could go home."

"You will." As if I had any right or authority to be making promises like that. "Even if it's not today or tomorrow, you two will go back to how things were before."

"No." She shook her head vaguely and got to her feet. "I don't think so." Tossing the handful of gravel she'd been holding onto the lawn all at once, she turned back toward the house. "I'm going to my room now, all right?"

"Sure. If you want to talk later, I'll be around."

She smiled, but I got the feeling it was more for my benefit than anything. "Thanks, Uncle Roger." I sat still on the steps for a few more minutes, watching the shadows from the garage and the awning get longer. How could things possibly be getting worse every single day? How could we not catch a break for even a minute?

When I went inside, I planned to head to my room, but my older brother's voice echoing from down the hall stopped me. What was he doing in Dad's office? Were they fighting? That wouldn't turn out well for anybody. I tried to make my way to the office quietly, but when I got closer, I realized that it wasn't actually an argument. At least not with Dad.

"No, by all means," Royce was saying, his voice tense with false politeness. I stopped outside the closed door to listen. "Tell me what the concern is. Is it our credibility? The publicity? What is it about this situation you think we aren't capable of handling?" There was a pause, so I figured he must be on the phone. He scoffed.

"Yes, and you'll notice that most of that has died down already because of *my* efforts. If anything, this should make it clearer how untouchable we are. But if you still need me to prove that we know what we're doing—" Another pause. "That's what I thought. So there's no longer an issue? Good to hear. We'll be in touch." I cringed slightly at hearing that from him, that line Dad only ever used as a vague threat.

After a few seconds of silence, I knocked at the door, and Royce snapped, "What?" When I opened it, the defensive anger on his face gave way to relief. "Roger. Hey. Uh, do you need something?"

"Just wanted to see how you're doing."

He looked just as ragged as the last time I'd seen him, if not more, and he let out a weak laugh. "It's been frustratingly easy to fit right back into all this," he said, gesturing to the office as he sat down at the desk chair. Unlike Dad, he didn't look like he belonged there at all. "I remember how it goes, the part I'm supposed to play. And I'm still good at it. Maybe that's a good thing, since..."

"Since me and Myles couldn't do it?"

"Don't say that like it's an insult. It's a shitty skill to have." He sat back in the chair and scrolled through something on Dad's laptop. "Where have you been all day?"

"Oh." Keeping it from Dad was a given, but surely it was safe to tell Royce. "I was at the safe house. With Jill." He looked up at me, eyebrows raised.

"Well, at least one of us is having some fun." There was a note of bitterness in his voice. Or maybe it was jealousy. "How is she? I have to say, when I saw her the other day, she didn't seem as angry as Myles was suggesting."

"It comes and goes," I laughed. "I think she's getting over it mostly, at least when it comes to me. At least she knows by now that I don't want her to be unhappy."

"And?"

"And what?"

He leveled a look at me over his glasses. "Don't give me that. You and I both know how you were after the two of you split up. And you practically begged me to help you make things right with her. You wouldn't do that if it weren't important to you. I'm asking if you've told *her* how you feel."

"Uh, not yet," I muttered, looking intently down at my shoes. "Not explicitly, anyway. I mean, she knows I missed her and how glad I am to see her again. She mentioned that she feels the same way. But we still disagree on some things. I feel like if I tried to tell her, she'd give me an ultimatum that I'm not prepared to meet. She keeps talking about me getting away from the family, just running off or something, and I have to keep explaining that I can't."

"What?" There was palpable outrage in his tone.

"She's just saying it because she knows it would be easier for me. She doesn't get how—"

"No." Royce shot to his feet and leaned forward against the desk to stare me down. "Why did you tell her you can't?"

"Wh—because you and Whitney and Myles would still be here?" Where the hell was this anger coming from? Why would he *want* me to leave? "And it wouldn't be right for me to get out of it while you—"

"Are you really that fucking stupid?" he demanded. "Don't you want to get out from under Dad?"

"Yeah."

"You want to be with Jill?"

"Of course I do, but—"

"And she wants to be with you? Away from here?"

"I think so."

"Then why the hell would you turn her down?" The way he looked at me, wide-eyed, incredulous, it was like he couldn't believe what an idiot I was. Usually a look he reserved for Myles.

"Because it would be turning my back on my family! I would be leaving you to keep dealing with Dad's shit, acting like it doesn't matter to me, like I don't have any responsibility to help you."

"Responsibility." He shook his head and reached up to pinch the bridge of his nose. "That was the word he always used, wasn't it? When we were growing up, learning about the business; it was our 'responsibility' to make sure it was successful. That's what I was thinking when I told Margot I couldn't leave to be with her full-time in Bristol. I had a responsibility to my family—no, specifically to my dad— and that took precedent over my responsibility to myself and my wife and my child. You think Dad ever thanked me for that? You think that sacrifice helped you or Myles in any way?"

Again, I was having trouble looking him in the eye. He had a point so solid that my reasoning looked flimsy next to it. "You can't change the way he is, Roger. You being here to share the misery isn't helping anyone. If you have the opportunity to leave, for God's sake, fucking leave!"

I swallowed hard. "And what happens when he tries to drag me back? The same way he dragged you back?"

"He won't," Royce said with a rueful smile. "As long as he has me and Whitney, he has the family's future all set up. He might even tell people he got rid of you because you couldn't hack it. You should wait until Jill's family has paid their debt, but after that, walk away."

I nodded slowly, trying to let myself think of this as an actual possibility. I'd been dismissing the whole idea for years, ever since that stupid shit I pulled on Justin Lawn. The violence was just a part of me, I figured, one I couldn't get away from. But like Jill said, that was the easier choice. Glancing up at my brother again, I managed, "Thanks. I'm gonna..."

"Yeah, go ahead." He smiled at me briefly before sitting down again and turning his attention back to the laptop. "I've got plenty more to do here, anyway."

"You should talk to Whitney," I said before I could stop myself. Royce frowned.

"About what?"

"She thinks you're too busy for her. She doesn't understand everything that's going on, why everybody's on edge, and she thinks it's her fault somehow. You should let her know it's not like that."

"Yeah," he said with a nod, "I should. Thanks."

I got back to my room as quickly as possible, already

getting my phone out to call Jill by the time I pulled the door closed.

"Hey," she answered with a smile in her voice. "I didn't expect to hear from you so soon. Are things that boring over there?"

"No, I just..." I had to stop myself, realizing that if I just jumped into the subject, she might think I was lying or moving too fast. Where could I start? "I was thinking about you."

"That's nice to know. Good thoughts, I hope."

"Always." My heart was already in my throat as I tried to figure out how to word what I wanted to say. Should've thought about that before calling. "And it's not really an unusual thing for me. Thinking about you."

"Well, I've certainly been thinking about you a lot more often lately," she laughed.

"No, I mean before that." I should've told her all this in person. I should've realized earlier that I was being an idiot and looking at everything wrong. Better late than never. "I feel like I haven't made it clear how big a deal it is for me to be with you again. But I really need you to know how long I spent thinking about you after we broke up. I know, that was forever ago, and it doesn't seem like it matters much anymore—"

"It matters." Her tone had suddenly gotten a lot more serious. "Go on."

"We talked about it some the other day," I said, lowering my voice a little. "After everything that happened, after I got expelled, I wanted to talk to you, and I couldn't. Felt like I didn't deserve to. And then you were just gone, and I was fucking devastated."

"Me too," she said softly. I could imagine her, nervous,

biting her lip like she did. "It hurt so much to know I couldn't be with you."

"And that feeling didn't go away." I was sitting on my bed, hunched over resting my arm on my knee and hoping she could hear how much I meant every word. "I thought about you constantly. For years. Even when I thought I was finally over it, I saw you again and I remembered why I spent so long missing you."

"Why?" She sounded a little breathless. "Tell me." *Now or never.*

"You know why. I loved you. And." I had to take a deep breath to steel myself. "And I think I still love you."

"Mm, Roger," she whimpered. "God, why are you telling me all this over the phone? If you were here right now..."

"What?" My voice got a little lower, a little rougher from that moan in her voice. My head was reeling from finally telling her what I'd been thinking every time I'd seen her the past few days, and I knew exactly what I wanted to focus on. "What if I were there?"

"Oh, I-I don't know," she muttered, suddenly getting shy like she did last time the subject was brought up.

"No, I'm curious now," I teased, hoping I could make her more comfortable. "I mean, thinking about what you did yesterday, I can kind of get an idea. But it'd be better if you told me yourself."

"Well." She hesitated for a second before deciding to give it a try. "I think after all that, you at least deserve a kiss."

"Yeah? So you can suck on my tongue again?"

Jill let out a nervous giggle. "Did you like that?"

"More than I expected to. Just made me think about everything else your mouth can do." And there I was thinking about it again, about her blushing and that little smile on her lips. "But I haven't gotten to show you what *my* tongue can do yet."

"Y-your tongue?" Excitement pitched her voice a little higher as she asked, "What do you mean?"

"I'm talking about eating you out, babe. Have you never...?"

"Um. No," she mumbled. "But now that I'm thinking about it, that sounds really good."

"Why don't you play with yourself while I tell you just how good it is?" I suggested.

After a second of hesitation, she sighed, "Okay." I went ahead and turn the lights out in my room, then got comfortable in bed to focus on her.

"You know you like my mouth on your neck," I told her, "how good my tongue feels there. You remember how I used to leave marks all over you because you liked the feeling so much?"

She whined quietly. "Yeah. And I liked having them."

"Then think about how we'd sit in my car during football games. How excited you got knowing somebody could catch us," I reminded her, recalling every detail myself and using them to get us both worked up. "You worried about taking your shirt off, so you'd just let me play with your tits underneath it. Remember?"

"Uh-huh." Her voice was starting to get a little husky too, and I could picture the hazy look in her eyes. "Then you figured out you could lay your seat back, and I'd let you push my shirt up so you could suck on them."

"And you liked that even more. You always liked kneeling over me like that," I teased, and she moaned again in embarrassment.

"It was a good position for you to touch me."

"Hang on, don't get ahead of me," I laughed. "Instead of

me finger-fucking you, think about me pushing you down on your back. Leaning over you and kissing down your stomach to your hips. My lips and my tongue on your hipbones."

"I would get ticklish," Jill laughed breathlessly, "and try to get away."

"Yeah, but not for long." I unzipped my pants and started lazily stroking myself while I was setting this scene for her. "Because I'd push your skirt up and lick you through your panties."

"What panties?" she teased, surprising me with another shock of heat.

"A skirt with nothing underneath? You were just waiting to get fucked, weren't you?"

"Well, I knew I was going to be with you. And you could never resist for very long when we were alone."

She had me there. "Then I guess my tongue on your pussy is your reward for coming prepared. It's totally different from my fingers. Softer. Hotter. A lot hotter." She moaned in my ear, so I took it further. "Think about me licking all over your clit and how wet you'd get." Thinking about all that was getting me hard faster than I expected, so I had to slow down my hand to concentrate. "Then my tongue going inside you."

"Oh, Roger," she panted. I could hear her breath steadily by that point.

"All I can think of is how good you'd taste," I told her, wetting my lips. "How hot and tight you'd be. And the sounds you'd make while I fucked you with my tongue."

"Mmm, please!" It sounded like she was really getting into it, her voice airy and shaky. "Please. I want you... inside me when I cum." *Christ.*

"Why don't you ride me then, babe?" Lying on my back,

I licked my palm wet and reached back down to stroke myself. "You want it so bad, come get it."

She let out a deep groan like she was frustrated—or maybe impatient. "I do want it. I want to sit in your lap or on your hips. And feel how deep you go. And you can just lie back and watch."

I was losing track of my breath too, thinking about her resting over me, her hands on my chest while her hips rolled and ground against mine. "Mm, that's it, babe. Fuck yourself on my cock, just like that."

"Ooh, God." Her breathing shuddered a little. "Roger, please. Tell me you're close. I. I want you to cum with me."

"You keep talking like that and I will," I promised, pumping faster and thinking about that desperate look on her face when she was close to cumming. "Tell me it's good. Tell me you like it."

"I... I like it," she managed. "Don't stop! Mm, you're so good! I want you to cum for me, baby."

"Fuck yeah, that's what I like to hear." I could barely hold on to my phone from getting so wrapped up in my fantasy. Her brown eyes and that smile she'd give me when she knew she was doing a good job. Her voice in my ear. Knowing she was getting close. It was too much. "Shit. I'm gonna—" I moaned out loud as I came, and I heard her tell-tale high-pitched whine about a second later. The thought of her cumming around me like she did the other night just made me even hotter. As I was trying and failing to calm down, I heard a soft, breathy laugh coming from my phone, and I realized I'd dropped it on the bed.

"Mm, what's funny?" I asked once I'd caught my breath enough to speak.

"I just... I didn't expect that to work so well," she giggled.

"And you were worried."

"Well, I did feel a little silly at the beginning. But it turned out okay."

"I love you," I told her quietly, and she let out a kind of dreamy sigh.

"You should get here earlier tomorrow," she said. "I want to see you as soon as possible."

"Oh. About that. Uh, there was something else kind of important I wanted to tell you." I forced myself to my feet and groped for the lights so I could clean myself up. "I got a little distracted."

"Haha," she said, and I could see her rolling her eyes. "What is it? You are still coming to see me, right?

"Well, the thing is, I want to get you out of there."

"Out of here? You want to move me again?"

"No, Jill, I want to take you home. There's no reason for you to be out there," I said as I sat back on my bed, fully dressed again. "And I was thinking. Maybe I could go with you." There was silence on her end, and I held my breath waiting for her answer. What if she thought that was a step too far? What if she'd decided she didn't actually want to keep seeing me?

"You're serious?" she asked.

"Completely."

"But. But I thought you said you couldn't," she reminded me. "You said you'd feel like a traitor. What about Royce and Whitney and Myles?"

"I actually talked to Royce about that. He encouraged me to leave. I mean, me being here isn't making it any easier on them. It's just giving my dad another target. And even if I left, I might still be able to help them deal with him." I was talking out the explanation as much for myself as for her. "I don't have to leave San Diego. I don't have to cut ties completely. I'm not enough of an asset to the business that

Dad will expend resources to keep me around." Again, a few seconds passed in silence. "So I was thinking, if I could have a few days to work everything out, make sure Royce and Myles are okay, separate myself from all my dad's accounts, then I could leave when you do."

"It almost sounds too good to be true," she said thoughtfully. "I mean, it does sound great. It sounds perfect. It sounds like exactly what I wanted. But I'm worried that you made the decision so suddenly. What if it doesn't work out like you're imagining?"

"It'll work out. One way or another. I'll make *sure* it works out. We'll get away from all my 'family' bullshit, and things will get a lot easier. Trust me, okay?" Another moment of silence.

"Okay," she agreed finally. "I trust you. But keep in touch with me, okay? I hate being in the dark out here. I want to know things are going all right."

"I will. I'll call you tomorrow and update you again."

"Okay. Good night, Roger."

"Yeah. Good night."

I ended the call and took a deep, slow breath. Jill's uncertainty was understandable, but I was going to prove to her that I could make this work. And then, if I could keep up my relationship with her, if we could actually stay together this time? I couldn't think of anything I wanted more.

My phone's clock read 7:30, and I realized I was starving. Feeling good, a lot better than I had in a while, I started to leave my room—and found my dad standing outside. I stiffened and pulled away by reflex, and he smirked coldly.

"Having a nice chat?" he asked.

"How long have you been eavesdropping?" The thought that he might have heard me dirty-talking with Jill made my stomach turn.

"Just the past couple of minutes. I saw you and Royce had a very interesting conversation earlier, so I felt like you and I should have a talk too." Seeing the confusion on my face, he looked at me like I was an idiot and explained, "Do you think I don't have surveillance in my own office, son? You really know that little about how I do business?"

"What do you want to say?" I asked, refusing to let any fear show on my face.

"Come down to my office," he said, turning to lead the way. "It'll only take a minute."

14

JILL

After three full days of silence, I was a nervous wreck. Roger had told me he would call the next day, but I spent all day glancing at my phone, checking to see if I'd missed a call, and there was nothing! The first day, I was angry. Of course, his promise to "make sure it works out" wasn't one he could keep. He didn't have that kind of power. The least he could do was call me and tell me what was wrong, though.

The second day, I started to worry. What if his dad had found out he was trying to leave? Surely he wouldn't have his own son hurt. Or worse. Right? But he could be in captivity, just like I was. He could be locked up somewhere, and I would never know it, because no one would come to tell me. I tried my hardest not to assume the worst but found myself calling him more and more frequently throughout the day, leaving distressed messages, begging for him to get back to me.

By the third day, I was positive he was kidnapped or worse. There was no way he would willfully leave me in the dark for that long right after I'd specifically asked him to keep me updated. I spent the day trying to call him until I realized with horror that my phone was dying. I didn't have a charger! I immediately stopped using it but kept it in my hand at all times, praying for it to ring and for Roger's voice to come from the other end. It didn't happen.

That night, I finally noticed headlights coming up the road. I jumped to my feet and ran to the window, peeking out the blinds and looking for Roger. It was too dark for me to see what kind of car had pulled up, but once it was parked and shut off, three figures stepped out of it. None of them looked like Roger.

I took a few steps back from the door, going from relieved to terrified in seconds. When the locks turns and the door opened, my blood went cold. Deron Moretti. What was he doing there? What did he want from me? Had he gotten impatient with my dad already? I thought back to Myles's "joke" about losing my fingers. The two men with him were ones I didn't recognize, bodyguard types in black suits and sunglasses.

"Hello again, Miss Johnson," Deron said with a polite nod, hands in his pockets. He took a look around the room, first at the pile of books still on the island, then at the left-over takeout I'd been picking at, and finally at the expensive clothes Roger had bought me. "Well, my son has obviously been very busy here. Was he bringing you more little gifts every day?"

"We had lunch together," I said cautiously. "Twice." As much as I wanted to be defiant and gutsy, I had no idea what was going on; for all I knew, Deron was there to kill me and drop my corpse at my family's doorstep. Trying not to think of that, I asked, "Where is he?"

"Oh, I'm sure you would like to know." Still, he was totally casual, like there was nothing weird about this scenario at all. He glanced into the living room, then went to sit in one of the armchairs across from the sofa. "Have a seat. There's just a thing or two I'd like to discuss."

Despite my wariness, I did what he said, keeping my eyes on him at all times. "I'm listening."

Deron folded his hands in his lap, his posture staying perfectly straight. "You know, I'm really not sure what it is about you that feeds that obsession of his. How, after all this time, you still have him wrapped around your little finger."

"I don't know what you mean." Did he think I was the one manipulating Roger? Sure, maybe I had considered doing that for a while, but it was long gone from my mind at this point. I genuinely wanted to help him now.

"I think you do. I heard the two of you talking the other night," Deron informed me. When I realized exactly which conversation he meant, my face burned with embarrassment and I suddenly couldn't meet his eyes. He threw back his head and laughed at me. "Oh, don't worry, I didn't hear anything sensitive, though I'm sure there's been plenty of that going on, all things considered." What the hell did that mean, *all things considered*?

"So what *did* you hear?"

"All his very idealistic little plans about 'getting away' from me and the business I've worked so hard to build. The business that's supported him his entire life, despite how ungrateful he's been for it." Behind his polite mask, I could see a glimmer of contempt in his eyes, as if he was blaming me for Roger being tired of his bullshit.

I swallowed hard, hoping my fear wasn't obvious in my eyes. "What did you do to him?"

"Oh, you've got me all wrong," he said with a wave of his hand. "I didn't do anything to him. He's perfectly safe and still free to go where he wants. I didn't lock him up to keep him away from you. We had a chat, and I gave him a task. That's it." He must have been lying. Otherwise Roger would have come back already—or at least called me! Or answered one of my many phone calls. Or something... "You need to let Roger go."

"What?" I drew back, blinking at him in surprise. "That's what this is about? You don't want him to be with me?"

"Yes, that's the long and short of it," he agreed.

"Why?"

"Put simply,"—he leaned forward in his chair— "I don't like you. You think too highly of yourself without much to back it up. You think you deserve respect without earning it. You're selfish and have no sense of loyalty to family. To name a few."

Fighting back a sneer, I answered, "You're really being that petty about this? You have to have control over your children to the point that you decide who they *date*?"

"You haven't heard the best part yet. I came to tell you, like I told Roger, that if you two split up, I'll freely and gladly let him walk away from my business. No strings attached. No debts owed. A fresh start, if you want to look at it that way." He stared down his nose at me, probably observing the distrust on my face.

"Are you serious?"

"Absolutely. Like he told you, himself: he's not business-essential. I can get by without his contributions," Deron explained, crossing his legs ankle-over-knee. "All you have to do is cut ties with him. And he'll be free as a bird." I couldn't believe it. There had to be some kind of catch he wasn't mentioning.

"If you're so willing to let him go, what does it matter to you whether he's with me or not?" This almost felt like a game, like a stressful, unpleasant game of us dancing around each other's words, each trying to get information the other didn't want to give. Only I was already at a huge disadvantage.

"Even if he's no longer a part of my business, he's still my son. My flesh and blood. He'll still be related to me in the eyes of the rest of the world; that, I can't change. But what I can't stand for," he said with a resentful sneer, "Is to see him end up with someone related to Fred Johnson. Someone with a coward's blood in her veins." Again, I had to fight myself not to snap at him.

"How dare you? My father isn't a coward," I growled, clenching my hands into tight fists against my thighs. "You're the one who took advantage of him when he was desperate!"

Again, Deron laughed, though this time it felt even more ridiculing. "Oh, you naïve, ignorant child. You still don't know the full story, do you?"

"I know you're a monster who can't even treat his own family like human beings," I hissed despite my efforts to resist his taunting. "And I know you're not above lying and manipulating to get what you want, no matter who the victim is." Still, his smile didn't fade.

"Listen to me, Miss Johnson, just a few minutes without interrupting, and we'll see who's actually a 'monster.' Though I'll admit, I'm going to enjoy this." He got up from his seat and started to pace slowly back and forth in front of the coffee table. "Let me tell you a little story about your dear old dad. First, the reason his family was in debt: a gambling addiction he probably never mentioned to you."

"Liar."

Without missing a beat, Deron took a step closer to me and raised his hand, causing me to flinch away. But he didn't hit me, and when I looked up, he smiled coolly.

"Don't interrupt me again. Now as I was saying." He continued his pacing. "A gambling addiction that put him, his wife, and his two beloved daughters hundreds of thousands of dollars in debt. He made mistakes, sure, but he somehow had it in his head that more gambling was the answer. He was wrong, of course.

"When he finally realized just how bad his situation had become, he tried finding loans elsewhere—but of course, his pre-existing debt kept that from being a viable option. He would just be creating more problems for himself. So instead, he came to me. Being the generous man that I am, I often lend money to others who've made similar mistakes." He had his hands folded at his back while he talked, and he reminded me a lot of Myles when they'd first *presented* me in Deron's office. As much as they might have looked alike, though, I couldn't imagine Myles ever being this willfully cruel.

"But he was asking for a pretty significant sum, as you're now aware. As much as I like to assume the best of people, I am a businessman, and in my line of work, assuming the best of people gives them the opportunity to fuck you over. So, 'Fred,' I told him, 'I'll be happy to lend you the money you need. Being a father myself, I understand how important it is for a man to provide for his children.'" He was smirking now, as if he was enjoying putting on this elaborate performance even though we both knew it was bullshit.

"'But I'll need you to do something for me. Let's call it insurance.' Of course, he was desperate, so he agreed without asking exactly what the favor was. But I made it clear for him, anyway. In order to prove that he understood the gravity of the situation, I needed your father to take a man's life." He paused in his pacing and stared me down, watching for my reaction.

"Wh... what?" I must have misheard. He couldn't mean what I thought. And if he did, my dad would never have agreed to it.

"It's a standard condition of all loans I give out in amounts of a million or more. How else will I know I can count on them to repay me? Unless I hold a bargaining chip that can utterly ruin their lives? And the lives of everyone close to them, of course." He was still watching me intently, but I couldn't look up at him anymore. This was enough of a shock that I had officially lost my nerve. "I made sure he understood exactly what I was asking for. He would kill an enemy of mine, and I would gather irrefutable proof that he was guilty. Then I would keep this proof until his debt was paid off. And he did it, Miss Johnson. Your father killed a man because he needed money so desperately. To support you."

It was too much. It was all too much to accept at once. My dad? My sweet old dad who always tried to talk things out with reason? My dad who managed a grocery store and insisted on helping old women with their produce? He couldn't have. He couldn't, possibly. And if he had, it meant that every success we'd had in the past ten years—our new start in California, the store, my grand plans for the expansion—were all built on another person's death, probably a completely innocent person. *God.* I could hardly breathe. I could hardly think. And Deron Moretti laughed at the horror on my face.

Something stirred in me and urged me to attack him, to punish him for putting us in this position. I launched myself at him over the coffee table, trying to tackle him, to hit him, to scratch his eyes out. But he easily threw me to the floor, and his laughter didn't stop.

"You bastard!" I shouted, leaping at him again. "You're

the one who did this! It's all your fault!" One of his body-guards stepped forward to hold me back by my shoulder.

"You're giving me too much credit, Miss Johnson," he said on his way to the door. "Your father had a hand in it too." Once he was outside, the bodyguard shoved me to the ground and pulled the door closed behind them. I threw myself at it, yanking at the handle, screaming curses after them until they disappeared down the road. Losing my breath, I collapsed to the floor and started to sob. Until then, I hadn't even noticed the tears in my eyes. How was I supposed to move on from this? How was it the Morettis could always find more to take from me?

I wanted Roger there to hold me. I wanted him to tell me again that he loved me. Tell me his dad was lying, that my father wasn't guilty of something so horrible. That my entire adult life hadn't been supported by a murderer. Even if it was a lie, I wanted to hear it.

But if Deron had been telling the truth, maybe Roger wasn't even willing to see me anymore. Maybe he had accepted his dad's deal, the offer for his "fresh start" in exchange for cutting ties with me. No. He wouldn't. Just days ago, he'd told me he would fight to be with me. He'd said that he loved me. So why didn't I feel confident in that? Why didn't I feel confident in anything anymore?

15

ROGER

"I'm not too sick." The raspy roughness of my voice betrayed me while I argued with my mom, following her around her room. "I wanna go." It was a few weeks after my sixth birthday, and I'd been home from school the past couple of days with bronchitis. I definitely *was* still sick, but I was still trying to go with my mom to whatever social event she had planned for the afternoon. Anything was better than staying home alone with my dad.

"Sweetheart, you can barely talk," she pointed out sympathetically. "You need to stay at home and rest. Mina's making you chicken soup. You don't want that to go to waste, do you? It would hurt her feelings."

"I can eat it later," I argued. "I wanna go with you. What if... what if I get sicker while you're gone? What if I die?"

"Roger," she snapped, giving me a sharp look. "Don't say things like that. It's not funny."

"Sorry." I collapsed next to her vanity while she was putting on her earrings, and she let out a heavy sigh.

"My goodness, what a dramatic son I have," she said,

scooping me up into her arms. "It'll only be a few hours. Then I'll come right home and check on you."

"But I'm gonna be so bored. Dad's too busy to talk to me." She had been with me every day that I'd missed school, which was probably why I threw such a fit about her leaving.

She frowned and put her hand on my forehead. "Well..." she said cautiously, "you don't have *much* of a fever. Do you really feel like you're okay with going out?"

"Mm-hm!" That was a lie. I felt like garbage. But I hated the idea of being alone too much to acknowledge it.

"In that case, maybe—"

"Latasha." Dad stepped into the room and stared at us critically. "Shouldn't you be going? And Roger, shouldn't you be in bed?"

"Well, I was thinking of taking him with me," Mom said, holding me a little closer.

"What? He's sick as a dog. You can't take him to a party like that."

"It's a social function," she corrected, miffed. "Besides, maybe the fresh air will be good for him."

"No. He needs to rest, and if you don't leave soon, *you're* going to be late. Just leave him."

She frowned hard, and for a second, it looked like she might keep arguing. But since she was against it in the first place, she didn't bother. Looking down at me with an apologetic smile, she said, "Sorry, honey. Your father's right. You should stay here and get your rest, then you can go with me next time. Okay?"

Realizing that Dad was a lot less likely to change his mind than she was, I gave up. "Fine."

But there wasn't a next time. That was the day of her accident, a T-Bone collision that crushed her sleek sports car and killed her on impact. Not her fault. She did nothing wrong. She didn't fucking deserve to die. And if I had been with her, if my dad hadn't insisted on keeping me home, I would've been killed too. My survivor's guilt still haunted me twenty years later.

I pulled my car to a stop near an Italian restaurant called Il Giardino dei Piaceri. It was owned by another family like ours and had served as a neutral meeting place for mafia exchanges for years. People like my dad liked their traditions. I sat in the car for a few seconds, then slammed my hands into the steering wheel and sat back, pushing my hair out of my face.

Why her and not me? Why her and not me? Why her and not me?

I didn't know if I'd ever stop wondering, thinking about how much better off the family would be for her presence. What was I doing for them? How was I justifying being alive when she wasn't? I didn't have many exact memories of her, but that day was one I could never seem to shake.

What I was there at the restaurant to pick up, I wasn't quite sure. My dad hadn't specified, and I hadn't asked. An envelope. That was as much as I needed to know. Three days had passed since our "chat" and the deal he'd offered me.

"Stop seeing that Johnson girl," he said, "and you can go. I won't try to stop you. I won't even tell anyone you walked away like an ungrateful coward. We'll say it was 'mutual.' But you have to cut her out of your life. I know how you are about her. It's how you were ten years ago, too. You'll end up marrying her if she'll have you, and I can't allow that. I can't allow her and her pathetic family to be connected to mine. God forbid you should have a child with her." He sneered in disgust.

"And if I keep seeing her?" I asked, ready to challenge him, ready to fight him over this.

My dad took a deep breath and let it out slowly. "Then we both know what will happen. I'll end up making things difficult for you, and it'll be a lot of unnecessary grief for everyone. If you insist on being with her, I'll have to make it clear you're no longer my son. Meaning you'll no longer be under my protection. And I think there are some people who would be very interested in that information. Don't make me disown you, son. It doesn't look good for me either. Just get rid of the girl."

After several long seconds of silence, I agreed. I got surly and acted like it was a huge problem, but deep down, I was relieved. He'd said he would just let me go after this last task. All I had to do was give up Jill. And I *wouldn't*, obviously, not after everything I'd just told her, not after finally accepting how I still felt about her. But if I could make my dad think I was done with her, just for a few more days, I could get out of his reach before he found out I was still with her, and by the time he did, there would be nothing he could do to punish me.

Of course, that was all assuming he planned to go through with the deal. He generally kept his word on agreements like this one, maybe out of a sense of "honor," as if he had any. I just hoped that would apply to me too.

Once I'd taken a minute to breathe and push my feelings about my mom back into my memory, my apprehension about all this, I went inside and told the hostess I was looking for Mr. Nessuno. She nodded and led me to a booth at the far corner of the room. The man sitting there was around my dad's age, with dark gray hair and a walrus mustache. He sniffed loudly when I sat down.

"Moretti's boy, aren't you?" he asked. I nodded. These

exchanges usually happened silently, so it was odd that he was speaking at all. He reached into the inner pocket of his suit jacket—and old-fashioned suit like Dad wore, nothing flashy and fitted like Myles—and removed a thin envelope which he slid conspicuously across the table. It was a good thing everyone in this restaurant already knew what kind of place it was. Otherwise, he might have attracted unwanted attention. I took the envelope and put it inside my own jacket with another nod. But as I was about to get up, he spoke again.

"One of the older Moretti boys. That makes you Latasha's son, doesn't it?" For a second, I was torn about what to do, then I sank back down to the seat, watching him warily. Maybe out of respect or because they didn't want to upset me, people rarely brought my mom up when I was around. Since I was already thinking about her, I couldn't help taking the opportunity to talk about it.

"Did you know her?" I asked.

"I certainly did. Wonderful woman, your mother. Kinder than the sort you usually see in our circles." He folded his hands on the table and watched me with beady, unblinking eyes. "Heard her oldest just got back into town from an extended vacation."

"Yeah," I said with a frown. "You could say that."

He nodded slowly. "Real shame, what happened to her. Shouldn't have been done." Something about that wording seemed off to me.

"What do you mean 'done'?" He looked at me with something like pity in his eyes.

"Accidents do happen, young man. Every day. All around the world. What happened to your mother..." Glancing out the window at the street, he said, "I'm not certain that was an accident." My mouth went dry. What the hell did this stranger know about my mom or what happened to her?

"What." I swallowed hard and cleared my throat. "What makes you say that?"

"You learn things in this business, son. Maybe that means learning the difference between brake lines that are cut and ones that are worn down. Maybe it means knowing the difference between momentum and acceleration." He looked down at his hands thoughtfully, maybe remorsefully. "Or maybe it means having an acquaintance who insists he knows the 'reason' Latasha Moretti died. Difficult to say which will be useful in the long run."

"Wait, are you saying you know who did it?" My brain had practically stalled at the thought of all this, but I had to force it to catch up. This was too important to miss even a single detail. Our contact was already getting up from his seat.

"I don't know anything for sure. Don't have any proof," he said, "and I'm sure you're aware I can't just give out names. All I have is a strong hunch. Just a feeling. I figured you deserved to have at least that much too."

Even once he was gone, I couldn't force myself to stand. It wasn't like I'd never considered this a possibility. When you're a kid and your mom dies without warning, especially when you're a kid in my circumstances, you start thinking about every possible explanation for it. Trying to rationalize it any way you can.

Only it didn't make sense that anyone would deliberately kill her. Like the contact had said, she was an amazing person. She got along with everyone, no matter how hard they tried to resist it, so I couldn't think of any enemies she might have. Anyone who would stand to gain anything from her death. At the funeral, I'd been on the lookout for anyone whose grief looked fake, like I would find some kind of villain smirking at her casket and call them out. It didn't happen. In fact, everyone there was inconsolable except for—

Except for the one person you'd expect to be upset the most. The person who had just lost his wife, the mother of his children, who he supposedly loved. My dad didn't cry once. And sure, maybe that was because he sucked at expressing any emotion that wasn't anger. Maybe he really was just as fucked up about it as the rest of us, but in a quieter way. Thinking back about their relationship, I was started to form a different idea.

At the time, I was too young to completely understand what they fought about. Royce saw more of it than I did, and we'd talked about it plenty of times over the years.

If my mom was still around, she would be fighting him every step of the way.

And within a year of her death, he'd married Rena and started his new bunch of Moretti boys. Rena, who never argued with him, who was fine with being blissfully ignorant about his work. I didn't want this to be true. I didn't want to even acknowledge it as a possibility. But now that I'd started considering it, putting it all together, I couldn't let it go until I got a definitive answer.

16

JILL

Maybe after a week of it, I should've been used to my new wait-and-see circumstances, content to sit and read and wait and behave myself until one of the men showed up to give me a scrap of news.

I wasn't. Trying to stay informed, I'd been keeping an eye on the news and realized that the #MorettiMob trend had died down. Just like Roger had predicted. I hadn't seen any mention of them or me in days. Brooke still showed up regularly, but she'd been given other topics, none of which were nearly as serious. The Morettis really were completely beyond reproach. I wondered how many people they'd had to "shut up" this time. And how many of those voices were silenced forever.

I dwelled so long on what Deron had said about my dad that I wound up having nightmares about it and then not sleeping at all. My phone had finally died after my tenth attempt to call Roger. I was alone and utterly helpless until someone decided to come for me. As much as I wanted to believe that someone would be Roger, I was even having my doubts about him.

The following night, about twenty-four hours after Deron's visit, I was sitting curled up on the couch, staring down at the coffee table, unable to do anything but wait. Even when headlights shone through the curtains, my only response was to narrow my eyes a little against the glare. I was so shaken that I didn't have the will to be hopeful or scared. After all, it wasn't like I had any power in this situation; whatever my captors wanted to happen would be what happened. Some quiet, furious part of me railed against that thought, knowing it was defeatist bullshit just like Roger's. I told her to shut up and pulled my legs in tighter.

When the locks clicked, and the door opened, I looked up to see Roger step inside. Roger. Thank God. Seeing the state I was in, how fragile I was, he came to kneel beside the couch and take my hands. "Jill? Are you okay? I'm sorry I haven't been answering your calls; my dad had this stupid 'deal'—"

"I know." So he wasn't aware of Deron's visit to the safe house. "He came here yesterday and told me about it. He told me a lot of things, actually."

"What do you mean? What did he say?" He reached up to touch my cheek softly, rubbing his thumb over my cheekbone. Between that and the concern written all over his face, my brain must have realized it was safe to feel things again. As I started to answer him, I found my voice strained with tears.

"Did you... did you know about my dad?" I asked, holding his hand against my cheek but keeping my eyes locked on his. "What he did in New York. Is it true? He killed someone?" Roger's black eyes widened slightly, and he quickly looked away from me. "It is, isn't it? I've been trying so hard to tell myself it was a lie."

"I'm sorry," he said quietly. "I knew. But it never seemed like the right time to tell you."

"There would never be a 'right time.' There couldn't be. I don't *want* to know this," I muttered, squeezing my eyes shut tight. "All this time, I've been telling you how awful your family is. How they can't be trusted. But my own father is a liar and a murder. I wish I didn't know. I wish..." Shaking my head vaguely, I trailed off. There was no point wishing for things that couldn't happen.

"He was desperate, Jill. He was trying to take care of you and your sister. And he didn't talk about it in order to protect you."

"Don't tell me that," I said, jerking away from his hand and curling in closer to myself. "Don't. Your dad said the same thing. He did it to take care of us. That means I'm at fault too. And Annette and my mom. We all benefited from another person's death. All our happiness over the past ten years, all our ambitions—it's all poisoned now that I know what happened for us to get it." Tears were starting to make my eyes feel peppery, and I tried my best to wipe them away before they could surface.

"Please, I don't want to think about this right now," I told Roger. "You're finally here, and that helps. It helps so much." I kissed him gently, once, twice, and wrapped my arms around his neck. Still sitting on the ground, he let me crawl into his lap and held me close.

"Yeah," he agreed, "I'm here."

"I was really starting to worry that you took your dad's deal." I rested my head on his shoulder, running my fingertips along the seam of his shirt. "It's still unbelievable that he would be petty enough to try to break us up just because he doesn't like me."

"Only because you don't know him as well as I do. This

is the kind of shit he pulls all the time." His hand ran slowly up and down my spine, only making me relax against him more. "But I told you I wouldn't let that happen. The only reason I've been gone the past few days is so he wouldn't throw a fit before I could get away."

Somewhere behind his words, I heard "I had to make him think we're breaking up to make this easier for me, which is the reason I completely ignored you for four days straight." But I didn't want to fight with him about it. We would have plenty of time to talk about how bad solitary confinement was for my mental state later. Now that he was done working for his dad, we could see each other like a normal couple. No sneaking around. No unexpected absences. And after this radical shift in the way I saw my dad, I was even more grateful that I would have Roger there to support me when I confronted him.

"Can we go?" I asked, glancing toward the door. "You're done, right? 'Free as a bird.' So let's leave." I got to my feet, taking his hands in mine and trying to pull him up. "I'll introduce you to life as a normal law-abiding citizen. We can stay at my apartment for tonight. I swear, if I never see this place again, it'll be too soon." My attempts at lightening the mood didn't draw a smile from him like I'd hoped, and he resisted my tugging.

"Actually," he began, moving to sit on the couch, and I dropped his hands immediately.

"You're not going with me, are you?" I didn't want to believe it, but what other explanation could there be?

"Jill, listen—"

"Are you serious?" My head was spinning from being thrown around between so many emotions. But anger was the easiest one, so I held onto it tightly. "After all that talk about wanting to get away? After your big revelation and finally accepting that there's no point in staying, you still can't let it go?"

"There's something I still have to do here." His voice was painfully, infuriatingly calm. "And I can't do it if I walk away now. I want to leave it behind and be with you, but I can't *yet*. Just give me a little more time."

"How many times are you going to ask for 'a little more time,' Roger?" I couldn't even look at him, shoving both hands into my hair and grasping it to keep myself grounded. "How many times is there going to be 'just one more thing'?"

"This is important," he insisted, shoulders hunched in what looked like shame. "Not just to me, but to my whole family. They need me to—"

"God, your *family*," I growled. "I am so fucking tired of hearing about what your family 'needs' from you. I thought you were past this!"

"You thought I was past it? Past caring about the people who raised me and made me who I am?" From the edge on his voice, I could tell he was starting to get irritated too. By that point, I wanted a fight, some way to *act* on all the frustration I'd been dealing with for a week, so much that I was willing to goad him into one.

"You can be who you are without being constantly connected to them, Roger. You said yourself that just caring about them isn't making anything better. Whatever very important thing you're trying to accomplish, did they even ask you to do it? Are you really so hung up on your 'loyalty' that you can't do anything for your own sake?"

"Don't act like you understand my 'loyalty,'" he snapped, finally getting to his feet. Despite him towering over me, I didn't back down for a second. "Ever since you got here, you've been telling me to ignore what my family wants in order to help *you*. So don't pretend you give a shit about them in the first place."

"We're not talking about them right now. We're talking about you. You are not your brothers or your niece. No matter what you've been taught all your life: you are not your family! And you aren't a traitor if you take a step back from them."

"They've done more for me than you know. Everything I have, I owe to them," he told me, like he still thought this logic was going to appeal to me somehow. "It's not easy to make a selfish choice when I know they need me. It's not as simple to let it go as you're imagining."

"It doesn't have to be simple. Or easy. That doesn't mean you can't do it." Again, there were tears making it hard to speak, but I ignored them. I came closer and grasped Roger's shirt in both hands. "I want you. I want you so much more than I expected to, so much more than I want to. I do, and you need to know it. But I can't handle being involved with all of them too. Just tell me you'll walk away from it, like you said, like you want to, and we'll both be so much better off."

He kept his gaze locked on mine for a few long seconds, then closed his eyes and lowered his head. "I can't."

"You..." Hadn't he said that he loved me? Hadn't we agreed this was the best option for both of us? *I'll make sure it works out.* I was right to worry he wouldn't follow through. No matter what he said, he was too afraid to leave his family. Too afraid to find out who he was without their influence. I was the one stupid enough to think he could. There was no point wishing for things that couldn't happen. "Of course you can't."

Still not looking me in the face, he reached into his back

pocket and pulled out my cell phone to offer it to me. "You can call someone to come pick you up."

"You're just letting me go?" I asked listlessly, still too mired in shock and hurt to put up my wall of anger. "Just sending me away?"

"You shouldn't go too far on foot." He ignored my questions, as if I hadn't spoken. "It's dangerous."

"What do you care?" I growled, snatching the phone from his hand. "If I'm not useful to your family anymore, what does it matter what happens to me?" I turned to leave, desperate to get out of his sight before my tears could surface, but he caught my arm to stop me.

"All I need is a little more time," he said, his voice low. "And for you to understand how important this is. I wouldn't stay if it wasn't. I wouldn't be willing to watch you leave if it wasn't."

"But you're not going to tell me what it is." It wasn't a question. If he'd planned to explain exactly what he needed to do, he would've done it already. But he didn't. Which told me it was just a bullshit excuse to put off leaving, probably something else his dad had asked him to do, something helpful to the business. And if he was more interested in that than in staying with me, I was obviously not as important to him as he'd said. "There's no way for me to understand if you won't explain. I'm done taking you at your word. I can't do it anymore." I pulled my arm away and headed for the door again.

"Babe—" He touched me again, and I turned around by reflex to shove him away from me.

"Stop! For once in your goddamn life, just accept the decision you made and move on." Before he could stop me a third time, I bolted from the safe house and into the darkness outside. I thought I heard him calling after me, but I ignored it. Once I was far enough down the road that I knew he wouldn't hear, I allowed myself a sob as the tears rolled down my cheeks. The glow from my phone's screen blinded me for a second, but I managed to tap Annette's contact despite the shaking of my hands.

"Jill?" Her answer was timid and breathy, like she couldn't believe it was really me.

"Hey." I tried and failed to manage a smile she could hear in my voice.

"Oh my God, where are you? Are you okay? Did they hurt you?"

"I'm..." Well, I couldn't honestly say I was okay. "No, I'm not hurt. They let me go. But I need you to come get me."

"Of course I will! Just tell me where you are. I'm on my way to the car. Keep talking to me, okay? I'm so happy to hear your voice." It sounded like she was on the verge of tears too. I had every intention of spending the entire night crying with her while I explained everything that had happened.

17

ROGER

I stood still in the doorway and watched Jill run, barefoot, down the road. She was so eager to get away from me she probably hadn't even noticed. I couldn't get over what she'd said, how there would always be just one more thing. Almost exactly what Whitney had told me about her dad. And even though I knew she was wrong, and this wasn't the same as anything I'd done for my family in the past, I still understood why she felt that way.

My original plan on the drive to the safe house had been to explain everything to her. Tell her about the contact I'd met, what he'd said about my mom. Tell her my suspicions about my dad and Rena, that I needed to find out exactly what had happened before I could leave. But the more I'd thought about it, the more I'd realized just how weak my reasoning was. All I had was a feeling, after all. A strong hunch.

And really, I knew it wouldn't matter. I knew that as soon as she heard I was breaking my promise to leave with her, she wouldn't be interested in the reason why. All she would see was me refusing to leave, giving her another reason to doubt me. And her reaction said I was right. I thought about going after her in the car, trying to get her to talk to me again or at least staying with her until someone showed up to help. But she'd made it pretty clear I was the last person she wanted to see at the moment, so I let her go. All I could do was hope she would be safe and that maybe she would be willing to let me explain later.

But I had to focus on finding out what had happened to my mom. If I gave up on it now or didn't get answers, then breaking Jill's trust in me would've been for nothing. I headed back to the house and looked for Rena. Between her and my dad, it would be a lot easier to intimidate her, and I'd definitely be able to tell if she was lying to me. If she'd had anything to do with my mom's death, I would find out. For a second, I considering finding Royce and Myles, telling them what I knew and asking them to help me find out the truth. But there was no point until I had something concrete to tell them.

I found Rena in her "sewing room" working on some kind of needlepoint project, her eyebrows furrowed and tongue between her teeth in concentration. As long as I'd known her, she had always been into every possible form of sewing, but it seemed like it was more about appearances than her actually enjoying it. She'd given me a handmade scarf for my twentieth birthday, because, "That's what moms do!" We both knew she wasn't my mom and never would be. We both knew I didn't think of her that way. But she tried.

It was hard to believe she could've been involved in any sort of murder plot, but I couldn't discount anything without investigating. When I opened the door, and she glanced up, her hot pink lips pulled into a smile. "Hi, Roger. Do you need something?"

"Yeah. I was hoping we could talk for a minute," I said as

I sat down on the sofa near her desk. She must have picked up on my dark tone, because her smile quickly disappeared.

"Of course. Is something wrong?" She put her sewing to the side and folded her hands in her lap. "You've been gone since this morning, and I was beginning to worry a little. I know, you're a grown man, so it's silly to get all worked up when you don't come home right away, but it was just so long!" I tried to gather my thoughts and put them together into an intelligible sentence while listening to her babble and watching her start to wring her hands. "If I'm being totally honest, I've been worried about you all week. Myles told me all about this business that's been going on with Jill. What an unbelievable coincidence that she's come back into your life after all this time! I was actually hoping we would get the chance to talk about that—"

"Do you know who killed my mom?" I demanded, stopping her in her tracks. It wasn't the smooth opener I'd been rehearsing, but with her talking nonstop, it was all I could get out. She took in a gasp of horror, and her hands flew up to cover her mouth, squared-off fingernails matching her lips.

"Killed...?" she repeated quietly, as if she was scared of the word itself. "Roger, why would you say that? Your mother was in an accident, a horrible accident. She wasn't killed by anyone."

"I'm starting to think that's not the case." I watched her closely, looking for any sign of dishonesty or defensiveness. "You and my dad got married pretty quickly after her death. And Gregorio was born pretty damn soon after that. So if there was anyone who benefited from it, it was you two." Tears started to fill her eyes, her face twisted into a mask of distress and pain.

"No," she breathed. "Please don't say that. I never wanted

any harm to come to her. Never." She paused, looking away from me guiltily. "I'll admit that your father and I were seeing each other for some time while they were together. We both knew that it was wrong, but I"—she let out a sob and then sniffled to control herself— "I loved him. And Latasha was so sweet, so kind to me! I hated knowing that what we were doing would hurt her.

"I begged Deron to tell her. To end things between them so that he could be with me. And he told me at first that Morettis don't do divorce, that it would reflect badly on him somehow. But I couldn't keep up that lie forever. I wanted a life with him, our own family, something real." She clasped her hands tightly again and stared down at them as her tears dropped into her lap. As hard as I was trying to stay cold and suspicious, she wasn't making it easy. "He told me he would talk to her. He said he would tell her he was in love with someone else and they needed to go their separate ways. And I knew even that would be difficult for you boys, but I thought surely she would be better off knowing the truth. But then, the accident..."

As one of Mom's socialite acquaintances, Rena had been part of the large crowd at her funeral. And she'd cried as hard as anyone else, maybe even harder—from guilt, I now realized. Not because she'd had a hand in my mom's murder but because of the affair with my dad.

"I was never glad that she died, though!" she insisted. "I swear. That wasn't at all what I wanted. I didn't bear her any ill will. And I wanted to wait a respectful amount of time before your father and I married. But by then, Gregorio was already on the way, and Deron said it would look worse if we weren't married. There were only so many options. Roger, I can't say how sorry I am for what happened to your mother. But I had nothing, *nothing* to do with it."

"I believe you, Rena," I said, sitting back on the sofa and shoving a hand through my hair. "I should've known better than to accuse you in the first place." She might not have been the brightest bulb in the drawer, but she didn't have a malicious bone in her body. Too bad I couldn't say the same for my dad.

Morettis don't do divorce. I remembered what a huge fit he'd thrown when Royce and Margot had split up. Just like he told Rena: it reflected badly on us, made us look weak or like we couldn't commit. Murder, on the other hand? That was apparently something our family could do all too well. And maybe he had resented my mom enough that he felt like she deserved it.

"You don't think..." Rena was wringing her hands again, staring with unfocused eyes down at the plush beige carpet. "You don't think your father would have done that to her. Do you? I knew they had grown apart, but she was still his wife. He loved her once. He wouldn't." She looked up at me with wide eyes, like she was suddenly afraid for her own safety if she were to piss him off or he found someone new. And I didn't blame her.

"I don't know. I want to believe he didn't. I want to believe the whole thing was an accident and I'm jumping to conclusions. But honestly: I don't." I forced myself to my feet. "Do you know where he is? It seems like my only option is to ask him upfront."

"No. I haven't seen him in a bit." Her voice was pitched a little lower, like she was no longer making her usual effort to seem cheerful. As I was starting to leave, she called, "Roger?"

"Yeah?"

"There's been a lot of talk around the house lately, since Royce and Whitney came home. I've been meaning to ask.

Are you planning on leaving us?" There was no condemnation in her voice, no anger or betrayal.

"I don't know. Yes." I heaved a sigh. "I don't know."

"I think if that's what you want to do, you should," she said, turning her chair a little more to face me. "If that's what will make you happy. Deron insisted it was necessary to the business for Royce to come back, and of course, Royce is very good at what he does here. He's definitely an asset. But he's also family. I know you three aren't my children, but I still love all of you; I hate seeing him so unhappy. He's made a very selfless choice, being here, to protect his loved ones."

Her smile was a little sadder than normal. It finally occurred to me that she wasn't completely ignorant about my dad's work; she was just trying to make the best of it. And it sounded like she might have tried to talk my dad out of bringing Royce back. "Jill is staying in one of the safe houses right now, isn't she?" she asked.

"She was. But I saw her earlier, and now she's on her way home."

"She left?" Rena looked genuinely upset by that news. "But weren't you two patching things up? I was hoping to see her start visiting again. I always enjoyed having her around."

"Well, we were supposed to—it didn't work out the way we were planning," I muttered. "She said if I stay here, she doesn't want anything to do with me." The words left my mouth before I could stop them, despite how much I wanted to keep all this to myself.

"Oh. I can understand how she might feel that way. It's not easy, always wondering if the man you love is going to come home or not. But I hope that you two can work something out. I remember how happy she made you before, and I always thought you two were good for each other."

"Yeah," I mumbled. "Me too."

"Oh, but I'm being nosy, aren't I?" Rena laughed. She picked up her needlepoint again and started to fuss with it thoughtfully. "I just want what's best for you, you know. There's so much ugliness in the world, and you've grown up around a lot of it. I think you've earned some happiness."

Still in the doorway to the hall, I opened my mouth and closed it again. She and I didn't have many one-on-one conversations like this, definitely not long ones on serious subjects. Listening to her talk like that was forcing me to consider what Jill had said before, about me being so distant toward her. Maybe that wasn't fair. Part of me felt like I should thank her, but I didn't know how.

"Ahem. I'll see you later, Rena."

"I hope so," she said with a smile, back to her usual bubbly self. I wandered through the house, distracted, trying to figure out what to do next. *Find Dad.* His office was empty; even Royce wasn't there. He wasn't in his room, either. Not playing poker or billiards with his Associates. Not smoking a cigar at the bar outside. He must have been out on a job or something, but he would come back sometime.

Plan B: find Royce and Myles. I went to Royce's room and knocked, but there was no answer. Outside Myles's door, I could hear the sounds of that video game he liked, so I figured at least someone was still in the house. I knocked and opened the door to find him on his bed like before, controller in hand.

"What do you want?" he asked flatly, not looking at me. And what I had to say definitely wasn't going to improve his mood.

"Do you know where Royce is?"

"He took Whitney out earlier. They're seeing a movie or

something, I don't know. Father-daughter time." He shrugged and rolled his eyes like it was a stupid idea. "Guy leaves the country for two years, and now that he's back, he's a fucking celebrity, *apparently*. Must be tough, having all that responsibility."

I tried to brush off the irritation at his immaturity. Pretty soon, we were all going to have to deal with some pretty serious shit together, so I hoped he'd be able to put all that jealousy and resentment aside. "Let me know if Dad comes home."

"What are you even still doing here?" he asked, pausing the game to stare me down. "I thought you were supposed to be riding off into the sunset with your former ex-girlfriend. Escape the mob, live happily ever after. Et cetera."

Choking out a dry laugh, I told him, "I think she's back to being my current ex-girlfriend at this point."

"Pff. Yeah, sure she is."

"What's that supposed to mean?"

"It means unless she's moving across the country again, you'll probably get another opportunity to talk to her. And she'll end up giving you another chance, because she always does. Always did before," he pointed out, leaning back against the wall behind him. "If she'd had the opportunity, I bet she would've even forgiven you for the whole jealous beatdown thing. She likes you too much to just cut you out."

"I don't know, she seemed fed up this time." Her line about accepting my decisions and moving on was pretty final. "I don't think she's giving me any more chances."

"Man, you're fucking stupid," he remarked casually.

"Thanks."

"*Listen*, you think she would've warmed up to you that quick if she was totally over you?" he asked, raising his eyebrows over half-lidded eyes. "Ten years is a long time to forget you cared about somebody, and a week is a short time for all those memories to come back. From what I hear, you two fell back into your old habits pretty quick. She was like that with me. She was like that with Royce. She knows us and she still cares about us and I bet she was grateful for the reminder. Remind her again."

"What do you care about it, anyway? It doesn't have anything to do with you."

"Ah, sure it does. It's not like anybody's relationship is totally separate from the rest of the family. If that was the case, Royce and Margot would still be together." He shrugged and spread his hands with a grin. "What can I say? I like Jill. She doesn't scare easy—unlike another certain sister-in-law of mine—and she's not shy. Plus I like you better when she's around. You're kind of uptight otherwise." He picked up his controller and started his game again. "Look, my point is: give her a minute to cool off, then go talk to her again. I dare you to tell me that doesn't work."

"Psychology, right?" I asked, and he threw me a smirk.

"You're catching on."

18

JILL

"Shit," Annette said for the third time in the past four minutes since I'd finished telling my story. I'd left out some of the graphic details of my relationship with Roger, but she knew most of what had happened. Getting it all out into the open, just having someone to talk to, was incredibly cathartic. And I was right; I had cried for a significant portion of it. By this point, I had no more tears.

"Yeah," I muttered dully, trying and failing to ground myself again. I was at home, in my tiny apartment, sitting on the bed with my sister and sharing an old pint of Ben & Jerry's. Two weeks ago, this would have been a great night for me. We would have been laughing and teasing each other, loud enough to irritate my downstairs neighbors. But things had changed in that short time. Now everything just felt dark and heavy.

"I kept trying to talk to Dad about the debt thing after you were gone," she told me, digging another chunk of chocolate out of melted vanilla ice cream. "But he wouldn't tell me anything. Like, he just shut down completely. I never even knew he used to gamble."

"There's a lot we didn't know about him, apparently." I hadn't told her the worst part. I couldn't. If anyone was going to say it, it was going to be him. In spite of Annette's insistence that Mom and Dad would want to know I was okay immediately, I begged her to give me one night to acclimatize to being back in the real world before I had to bear all their tearful relief and celebrations. I definitely wasn't ready to face my dad yet.

"And what about Roger?" she ventured carefully, eyeing me like I might snap at her. As if I had the energy. I was already so drained that the thought of Roger barely brought back all the rage and despair I'd been through earlier.

"What about him?"

"It sounds like you guys were really enjoying seeing each other again. Like you were really happy being around him. And now you're just done with him? Just totally done?" She actually sounded sad about the idea. Maybe she really was excited to hear that I was letting myself have feelings for someone again.

"I gave him a choice. He knew how I felt about his family and their 'business.' And I told him, very clearly, that if he could leave them, I wanted to be with him. I did. But he couldn't do that. No matter how many times he told me he wanted to or how much he claimed to care about me, in the end, he was still too attached to them. So yes, I'm done." I ate another bite of brownie batter and dropped my spoon into the mostly empty carton.

"You mean with the ice cream, or...?" She could barely conceal her smile, and I rolled my eyes.

"Haha."

"But really. I wish it didn't have to be like that. I always liked Roger," she said. "He was nice."

"How do you even remember that? You were like, five."

"I was eleven," she corrected indignantly.

"Oh, right, practically an adult, then."

"Old enough to have memories." She stuck her tongue out at me. "Like he kept Myles from picking on me at school. He kept tripping me in the hall, and Roger was like 'that's no way to treat a lady' and made him apologize." I forgot sometimes that she and Myles were about the same age; he'd seemed so much older, somehow.

"If you can believe it, Myles is even more of a brat now."

"Yeah, that's what it sounds like," she laughed. "It's just weird to think about how things turned out. How we all used to be really close: you and me, Roger, Myles, and Royce. Like, I was already thinking of Roger as my big brother when—"

"Annette," I said, lying down on my back and closing my eyes. "I don't think I can talk about this anymore tonight. I'm going to have to tell the whole story again for Mom and Dad tomorrow, so can I have a break? Can we talk about something else?" She was reminding me way too much how familiar the Morettis were, how much I had cared about all of them. In the past.

"Sure. Um, but I don't really have any good news." She told me about the store, how the Escondido location had totally stalled without me. With all the publicity after I was kidnapped, they'd gotten a lot busier, and Dad was having a hard time managing all the extra customers and busybodies trying to see what they knew about the mafia. Definitely no good news. But it didn't bother me as much as I expected. Maybe because I was too tired to be bothered. Maybe because I couldn't look at the store, the same way anymore after everything I'd learned.

～

THE NEXT MORNING, after much stalling under the pretense of "enjoying being back home," I finally let Annette drag me to Mom and Dad's place. It was the house we'd had since our move to San Diego, not huge or crazy like the Moretti properties, but modest. When we rang the doorbell and Mom answered, she took one look at me and immediately burst into tears. Dragging me into a hug, she sobbed into my hair while I patted her back and tried to tell her there was nothing to worry about, that I was okay. She called for my Dad, who quickly came downstairs and had a similar reaction when he saw me. I was less receptive to his hug.

"My God, Jill," Mom said, cupping my face in her hands, still crying steadily. "Where were you? What happened?" We went into the living room, and I sat in the middle of the sofa with Mom on my left, holding both my hands, and Annette on my right. Dad stood nearby, seeming anxious to hear the story. Probably worried I had found out his secret.

In this version of the events, I left out my rekindled relationship with Roger altogether. Annette looked at me a little funny when I skipped over those parts, but I shot her a warning glance and she stayed quiet.

"But they didn't hurt you?" Mom asked when I had finished. "You seem so exhausted, honey. Were they feeding you?"

"I had food, Mom, don't worry. It was just spending all that time alone that really f—messed me up. Feeling so helpless." Shaking my head, I muttered, "That was the worst part."

"The police came to speak with us," Dad told me, "after your friend put that video from the store on the news." My friend. Brooke. Yet another thing I had weird mixed feelings about.

"They actually seemed kind of excited," Annette said.

"Like having the video proof was a big deal and they would finally be able to arrest the Morettis or whatever."

"But of course, it didn't work out that way." The look on Dad's face was sour and bitter at the same time. "Deron Moretti is too powerful for a little thing like kidnapping to bring him to justice. I always knew those people were bad news."

"And you still went to them for money," I blurted without meaning to. "Let's not pretend like Deron Moretti is the only person who's done anything wrong, Dad." I just couldn't stand sitting there, listening to him act sanctimonious after what he'd done. His eyes went wide when I snapped at him, and so did Mom's.

"What do you mean? Did someone else hurt you?" she asked. But Dad was caught in the hard glare I'd fixed him with. He could tell that I knew.

"Ahem. Jill, could I talk to you alone for a second, sweetheart?"

"No," I said flatly. "Let's talk here." Seeing him wince, I wanted to feel bad, but I couldn't.

"Is something wrong?" Mom asked, looking from me to him, then back again. Visibly sweating, Dad swallowed hard.

"I really don't think—"

"They deserve to know, Dad. The whole story." I wasn't asking. "I want you to be the one to tell them." After another moment of pleading with his eyes and the realization that I wasn't going to let this go, he lowered himself shakily into his old maroon recliner.

"I guess it was bound to come out eventually," he said, leaning forward against his knees and clasping his hands. "I should've been honest with you all years ago."

Between his hesitation and our questions, it took about

an hour for him to get through the story. Mom was crying by the end of it, covering her mouth with one trembling hand and staring at him in disbelief. "Tamara," he started, reaching out to her, but she recoiled in horror, shaking her head. He must have seen the change in all three of us. Hanging his head, he muttered, "I'm so sorry. I know that nothing I say will change what I've done. I've been trying to raise the money to pay Deron off. So that none of you would have to know about this and it would just be my burden. But I don't have it. And I'm not sure Deron will be patient with me for any longer."

"What are you saying?" I asked. He took a deep breath and looked up at the far wall.

"I think it's time I turned myself in," he said, drawing another loud sob from Mom. Unable to look at him anymore, she turned to embrace me and buried her face against my shoulder. My right hand was still holding Annette's left tightly. "I know that won't make this any easier for you. But you aren't the ones who owe him. And he won't have any more leverage over me. This is the only way to end it."

If he thought being in prison would keep him out of the Morettis' reach, he was wrong. They must have had people even there; I got the feeling there was practically nowhere to hide where they wouldn't find you if they really wanted to. When I realized that my dad was going to die in prison, I finally started to cry and huddled with my mom and sister for comfort.

∼

THE POLICE CAME THAT NIGHT. As much as we'd hoped otherwise, they'd sent multiple cars after hearing all the details Dad confessed to. There were red and blue lights, uniformed officers, and plenty of neighbors outside to see what the commotion was about. We stood outside the house together while Dad followed instructions from the nearest officer, putting his hands up, walking slowly to one of the cruisers. They read him the Miranda warning, and even after being told that anything he said could and would be used against him in a court of law, he said loudly, "Everything I did, I did to help my family."

"Bullshit!" Annette shouted through her tears. Realizing that people were staring, she let out a frustrated growl and covered her face with both hands. "You think this is helping? You just screwed us over a different way."

THE NEXT MORNING, I got a call from Brooke. "Jill! I just saw that you're back home. What happened? How did you get away from the Morettis? God, I've been so worried."

I thought about her spotless composure during her many reports about the search for me. Just like Roger had pointed out, I wouldn't have described her as looking "so worried." But I reminded myself she at least deserved the chance to explain her motivation.

"Don't worry. I'm fine. They actually just let me go." There was a pause on her end.

"Do you want to talk about it? Could we maybe do lunch or something?"

"Are you asking as my friend or as a reporter?" She wasn't the first reporter to contact me, though most of them didn't have my personal phone number. Still, everyone was looking for the story of the Moretti hostage who had lived to tell the tale, a story I wasn't even marginally willing to share.

"Jill." Brooke sounded hurt by my question. "I've seriously been worried about you. I just want to know you're okay. It's fine if you'd rather not talk about it. I'd still like to see you, just to touch base. Is that okay?"

My time with the Morettis must have made me a little harsher. That wasn't her fault, and she didn't deserve my suspicions. "I'm sorry," I sighed, pushing a hand through my hair. "Yeah, I think lunch sounds great. After a week and a half in solitary confinement, it would probably be good for me. Where do you want to go?"

A couple of hours later, we met at Crema Blanca, a bistro we'd visited plenty of times in the past for similar lunch dates. Brooke was already there when I arrived, and she quickly put her phone down to get up and hug me. "I'm so glad to see you. Hang on." She pulled away and looked me over, maybe inspecting for any visible injuries. "You don't *look* any worse for wear. Maybe a little tired." She touched my cheek, and I brushed her off to sit down.

"I'm fine. They didn't have me chained up in a basement or anything," I told her. "And they didn't beat me or starve me. It was the least intense hostage situation you can imagine, honestly."

"That's good to hear." She smoothed her dress underneath her as she sat across from me. "I ordered you a caramel macchiato; I hope that's okay."

"It's perfect. I haven't had coffee all week." I'd been right to think that going out would be good for me. Normalcy was nice. Just people going about their lives around me. Apparently, news of Dad's arrest hadn't made the rounds yet, at least not with my face attached.

"I still can't believe they just let you go," Brooke said, resting her chin on folded hands. "No explanation? No warnings or threats?"

"Nope," I lied. "Maybe they were tired of waiting for my dad to pay up. Maybe they were tired of me complaining."

"Oh, I hope you gave them hell," she said with a smirk.

"Something like that." *I actually gave one of them head.* I shook that thought out of my mind. Telling Annette about my relationship with Roger was one thing. Telling a friend who happened to be a journalist was something else.

"So where were you? I heard they searched the Morettis' house and there was no sign of you." Almost an exact quote from her report.

"Yeah, I heard about that too. For the majority of the time, they had me in this remote safe house out on a mesa somewhere." I gave her a wry smile. "I watched the news a lot out there, actually. I saw a couple of the reports you did on the whole story."

"Oh! Really?" She didn't seem to feel guilty for it at all. In fact, she seemed proud that I had caught it. "How interesting that they let you have access to something like that."

"Well, it's not like there was anything I could do with the information. They took my cell phone when I first got there," I explained. A server brought my coffee, and I thanked him with a smile. The first sip was so good I couldn't help sighing in delight. "Hmm, good choice."

"You weren't gone long enough for me to forget your favorites," she said. The detour was brief, though, as she quickly went back into her curiosity about my stay with the Morettis. "Did they ever talk to you? Or threaten you? Did you actually meet Deron Moretti?"

"Brooke," I said, leveling a look at her, "why do I feel like I'm being interviewed right now?" She blanched slightly and looked away.

"I'm sorry. It's just instinct, I guess. I'll stop, I promise." She crossed her heart and changed the subject. "Do you have any idea when you'll go back to work? Or have you thought about that yet?"

"Only a little." I was actually dreading going back. There was no way to know for sure until I tried, but I had the feeling that it would never feel the same as before. I would never love it as much. "I'm not sure exactly how to approach it, honestly. It's something to think about in a few days, once I've gotten settled again."

"That makes sense. But aren't there decisions that need to be made before that?" she asked. "With your dad arrested, that kind of makes you the de facto owner, doesn't it?"

Again, her questions were feeling very pointed. "You know about that, huh?"

"I have to know about everything newsworthy that goes on in town."

"Is that what it was? Newsworthy?" I asked, eyes locked on the red lipstick stain she'd left on her mug.

"Well, yeah. 'Mild-mannered fifty-year-old grocery store owner contacts police, confesses to a murder committed ten years ago across the country'? If that's not news, I don't know what is." She actually laughed at that, somehow not realizing that this was a *bit* of a sore subject for me.

"Right. I guess I'm having a hard time seeing it that way since I'm so personally involved."

"Speaking of 'personally involved,'" she said with a mischievous smile. "A little birdy told me that you and Roger Moretti knew each other before all this went down. Is that true? Be honest, now."

It was subtle, but I saw her turn her phone on the table so the mic end was facing me. Acting on a hunch, I snatched up her phone and found that it was, in fact, recording our conversation. I stopped the recording and put the phone back, fixing Brooke with a hard glare. She at least had the decency to look ashamed.

"Were you actually worried about me at all?" I asked. "Or was that just a convenient excuse to get me to tell you all the awful things I just went through?"

"Of course I was," she insisted. "My professional interest in what happened doesn't erase the fact that you're my friend. But Jill, you can't act like this isn't an incredibly important story."

"Important?" I repeated. "How so?"

"Maybe you don't know this because you aren't part of the industry, but it's insanely difficult to get any information on the Morettis to press," she said, picking up her cup and taking another sip. White chocolate mocha, if I had to guess. "I mean, dangerously difficult. The fact that you have an inside perspective? That you got a glimpse at how they work and how they live, then they let you go? *Alive?* That's a miracle! How can you justify keeping it to yourself?"

"So you're just trying to do your journalistic duty, right? Just trying to inform the masses?"

"As opposed to...?" she asked with a slight edge to her voice.

"I don't know, using my traumatic experience to get yourself some accolades? Using my trust in you as my friend to get information you know I'd rather not share publicly?"

She let out a frustrated huff, like I was being difficult and unreasonable. "Why is it so important to keep this information secret? Unless you have some kind of private personal stake in it." She was watching me carefully, and I hoped my emotional response to her prodding wasn't visible. "Or do you? Is that why you're so reluctant to share? Because you're a part of The Family now?"

I scoffed and rolled my eyes. "Why would they have sent me away if that were the case?"

"I'm not hearing a 'no,' honey." Leaning in closer, still scrutinizing my face, she went on, "That's it, isn't it? That's the reason you're being so cagey about the whole thing. You weren't actually there as a hostage; you were there as Roger Moretti's pet."

"Fuck you, Brooke," I hissed, pushing away from the table to get up.

"I don't want to say it if it isn't true," she continued. "I don't want to publish it if it isn't true. But if you don't give me some indication of what's true and what isn't, all I have are my journalistic instincts, and they're telling me your stay with the Morettis was actually *very* comfortable." Her not-so-subtle attempts at blackmailing me rolled off my back with no effect.

"I don't care what you say or what you publish," I told her, pulling my purse onto my shoulder. "Do whatever you want. And when you do, we'll both know that your 'journalistic instincts' amount to nothing more than a fucking gossip column. You're not discovering anything. You're not shining a light on the inner workings of the mafia. The bullshit you have to say wouldn't even be worth them shutting you up."

On the way back to my apartment, I found myself wondering why I had gotten so defensive about this. Maybe it was because I was still sore over my break up with Roger. I didn't want to admit I had feelings for him. Maybe it was about protecting my own emotional experience. Or maybe, some part of me wanted to say, I felt like giving out all the details of the Morettis' business would have been disloyal, somehow.

19

ROGER

For as long as I could remember, I had been afraid of turning out like my dad. After what I'd done to Justin, I started thinking that it was inescapeable. So I'd given in to his pushing for me to join the business. I'd followed his orders despite knowing they were wrong. I let him convince me that Royce was a traitor for trying to break away and live his life, for wanting better for his daughter. I saw all the lives our family had ruined and wrote them off as collateral damage. "It's not right, but it's how things are." Because I thought it was all I was capable of.

Jill knew that was bullshit. Deep down, I knew it too, but like she said, it was easier to just not question it. It was easier to be on the side with the power and pretend it was because I belonged there. But if it was true that my dad had been responsible for my mom's death, I couldn't accept that anymore. I couldn't accept anything that put me on his side, that condoned the way he did business or the way he treated others.

Mom tried to tell him when he was wrong. She tried to tell him he could be a better man, that the easiest option wasn't always the right one. And the fucking bastard had killed her for disagreeing with him. I wasn't going to be that person. I wasn't going to be the idiot who lost an amazing woman because he refused to change. Because he was afraid of looking weak. No way was that important enough to give her up over. I just hoped telling her that would be enough to get me another chance.

Jill had told me about her tiny apartment. I knew that it was in North Park, at least, a busy area in downtown San Diego with a high population density. How many apartments could there be in that area? I refused to use our family's resources to find her. Instead, I went there myself and walked the streets, looking for places like she'd described. She mentioned a fountain she would see from her bedroom window. That narrowed it down some. Then I looked for places with one-bedrooms on the eighth floor. Of course, it wasn't easy to do all this research without getting a few weird looks, but I felt like it was important that I do it myself. No mafia shortcuts. Just extra effort. At least, I hoped that would win me some brownie points.

Even when I found the place, it wasn't like I could just go up to the eighth floor and start knocking on every door in the hall. I waited in the lobby and tried calling the number I'd gotten from her phone. She didn't answer. For a while, I paced the room, trying to decide how to proceed. The staff at the desk asked me multiple times if I needed help, and I couldn't tell them, "nah, I'm good, just waiting for my ex-ex-ex-girlfriend to come down so I can talk to her."

I wound up sitting in the lobby, hands folded, bouncing my foot nervously, for around two hours before Jill finally came in. She was digging through her purse and didn't see me at first, but when she looked up and her eyes met mine, she frowned hard.

"What are you doing here?" She asked coolly. I remembered Myles's encouragement. He thought she would without a doubt forgive me. The wary look in her eyes said it might be possible, but I was going to have to work for it.

"I was hoping we could talk." I kept my hands off her, kept from getting too close, since I knew how easy it would be for her to reject me completely.

"About what? I feel like our last conversation made things between us pretty clear," she said, arms crossed.

"It's about that, actually. I want to explain myself."

She let out an impatient sigh. "What's there to explain, Roger? Have you changed your mind *again*? I'm getting really tired of getting my hopes up that—"

"It's about my mom," I told her quietly, hoping that would be enough to at least make her listen. Her eyes blinked wide, then quickly narrowed again. I could see her calculating for a second before she let out a sigh.

"Come upstairs," she said, leading me to the elevators. I followed at a respectful distance, trying not to make any assumptions about whatever was or wasn't still between us. Despite us pretty effectively breaking up the last time we'd seen each other—if we were together in the first place—my first thought after everything I'd learned about my mom's death was that I wanted to share it with her. I had plans to meet with Royce and Myles that afternoon to tell them, which was going to be a shitty experience without a doubt, but I felt like it would be ten times easier with Jill there.

When we got up to her place, I saw that the word "tiny" really wasn't an exaggeration. This was where she lived? It couldn't have been more than four hundred square feet. How much did she get paid working at their store...? I found myself thinking about how I would do better for her. If she would let me.

"Are you telling me the reason you had to stay, your 'one last thing' had something to do with your mom?" Jill asked, setting her purse on the kitchen counter and sitting down on the loveseat in the living room, which was basically the same room. When she saw me awkwardly standing near the door, she sighed and scooted to the far end of the loveseat, nodding to the other side so I could sit down.

"Yes. My dad gave me a pickup task, but the contact who was there apparently knew my mom." I told her everything I'd learned, starting with the hint from the contact, then my speculation and the conclusion I'd come to about my dad and Rena. The conversation I'd had with her and everything she'd explained. How I was positive now that my dad had something to do with my mom's death but didn't have any hard proof yet. How I was planning to tell Royce and Myles next.

"Wait, so you told me about this before you brought it up to your own brothers?" she asked, wide-eyed.

"It's going to be hard for them to hear. They're going to want to do something about it right away, I'm sure. I... maybe I was hoping to talk it all out and give myself a second to breathe," I admitted, staring down at the gaudy rug under her coffee table. "I know, it doesn't really involve you, so maybe I shouldn't have bothered you with it."

"Don't say that. I understand how important this is to you," she said, moving closer to put her hand over mine on my knee. "If talking to me about it helps you at all, I'll listen. But why didn't you tell me this before? I would never have tried to stop you if I'd known what you were really doing."

"I guess I assumed you would want me to leave anyway," I said. "I thought you might say there was nothing important enough to keep me from leaving. Not even this. And I couldn't agree with that that. Not without finding out for sure what happened to her."

Jill shook her head. "I understand that. Of course I do. Next time, don't assume how I'll react. Just be honest with me about what's going on and let me give you a response."

"Next time?" I asked, turning my hand over to hold on to hers.

"You heard me. You already know I want to be with you. When you said you couldn't leave, I thought it was a choice you were making. I thought you were deciding that staying in your dad's good graces was more important than being with me. But this isn't a choice. It's not you refusing to branch out from what you already know. It's something you have to do. I can't fault you for needing to see this through, and if you have to stay with them to do it, then fine. For now." She curled her fingers around mine and looked earnestly into my eyes. "If I can, I want to help."

"Thank you." I leaned in a little, and she smiled as she closed the gap to kiss me.

"God," she muttered when she pulled away. "I knew your father was an asshole, but I never would have imagined he could do something so horrible to his own wife."

"Maybe it shouldn't surprise me. He only values people who are useful to him, and she was too much trouble. So much for fucking 'family.'" This was the same man who had always insisted blood was the most important thing in the world. But given everything else I knew about him, I probably should have expected that he was a hypocrite along with everything else.

"I'm sorry, Roger." Jill squeezed my hand, and the pain in her eyes was obviously genuine. "You'll talk with Royce and Myles. The three of you can confront him and get some kind of justice for her."

"Yeah." Not that punishing him would change anything. It wouldn't bring her back. But if he really was guilty, he had to pay somehow.

"My dad was arrested last night," she said out of nowhere.

"What? Why?"

She explained what had gone down at her parents' place the night before, how she had told him to confess what he'd done to her mom and sister, then he'd taken it a step further and turned himself in to the police. The way she explained it, detached and practically numb, only made me more worried.

"Are you okay?" I asked when she finished the story. She shrugged.

"I will be. It's already happened. There was no way for me to forget what he did or pretend I'm okay with it. All I can do is try and move on." Shaking her head, she went on, "But it doesn't matter right now. We need to talk to your brothers and figure out what to do about *your* dad." It seemed like we were both in pretty fucked up places with regard to our parents. But at least we would be able to deal with it together.

When I went back to the house, Jill came with me, keeping her hand in mine the whole time. Royce was already waiting in the conference room, looking better rested and less stressed than the last time I'd seen him. Seeing Jill at my side, he looked between us, then at our clasped hands, and smirked at me knowingly. "Feeling more comfortable here now that you're not a prisoner anymore?" he asked her.

"Only a little. You guys are still way too rich and extravagant for my taste," she said.

"Fair enough. But I'd like to go on record saying that I did not decorate this place."

Myles gave me a similar grin when he saw Jill there. "Told you so," he said, giving her a nod. "Do you guys have an *announcement* or something?"

"Not exactly," I told him. We all crowded at one end of the long table meant for ten or more people. "I want to warn you: this isn't going to be easy to hear."

"What, is it about you leaving?" Myles asked, leaning on one arm against the table and resting his chin in his hand. "I mean, sure, it's gonna suck, but it's not like—"

"Myles. I'm serious. This is a big deal."

"Just tell us what's going on," Royce said. I'd been trying to decide how to approach this, how to set it up, but there was just no easy way to do it.

"I met somebody recently who knew Mom. One of our contacts. And he told me her death wasn't an accident."

That statement sucked all the air out of the room, and there was silence for more than a few seconds while my brothers absorbed what I had said and exactly what it meant.

"How the fuck would he know that?" Myles demanded.

"Said he had an acquaintance who was in on it," I explained. "He wouldn't give me the name."

"Well let's fucking find him and *make him* give us the name! How could you just let him walk away?"

"People don't give away names easily in our circles, Myles," Royce pointed out, surprisingly calm about the whole thing. "Most of the people we work with could be tortured for weeks and still wouldn't rat. That's the whole reason we work with them. So what are we supposed to do with this information?"

"There's more," I said, sure that this would get an even

worse reaction. "I think Dad might have had something to do with it."

"What do you mean? You think he killed her?" Myles was beside himself with shock and denial. "He couldn't."

"Why not? Think about it: he married Rena less than a year after Mom died. She told me he was cheating on Mom with her. And he promised he would talk to her just before the accident. How many times did you see them argue?" I asked Royce. "And you said he would get *pissed* at her when they did."

"And he wouldn't have divorced her," he agreed slowly, eyes narrowing behind his glasses. "Rena is easier to deal with. And it isn't like he didn't have experience with this sort of thing. It would've been easy for him to arrange."

"Are you two fucking crazy?" Myles snapped, shoving to his feet. "Do you hear yourselves? You think he would do something like that just because she irritated him?"

"Yes," Royce said plainly. "It's what he's always done with people who don't toe the line. You can't possibly believe he genuinely cares as much about family ties as he says. He only plays the family angle when it's convenient to him; otherwise, it's all *his* work and *his* money and *his* business. He was willing to use Margot and Whitney against me. He's a self-serving piece of garbage. Yes, I believe he would kill her just because she was inconvenient."

Myles was breathing hard, staring down at the table with wide, desperate eyes, obviously struggling to accept this. "We have to ask him," he concluded. "We have to find out if he really did it."

"And if he did?" Royce prompted. I could feel the anger and outrage coming off him, but they were quieter than Myles's or mine. He wasn't looking at anyone by that point, his eyes directed at the tabletop but unfocused. "What then? What are we going to do about it?"

"Something," I said firmly. "Even if we don't know what yet, I think we can all agree that we can't just let this go. If I'm right, he's going to have to answer for it."

"How? He's practically untouchable," Royce said. "You think we can turn him in to the police? You think we can hire someone to 'take care of' him?"

"I think that's not the decision that has to be made right now," I countered. "Right now, we have to find out if we're even right about this."

"Then I guess we'll need to find some proof."

"Couldn't you just ask him?" Jill suggested, cautious about getting involved in the conversation. "I mean, you obviously know him better than I do, but he seems like the kind of person who owns all his choices. And if he thinks you can't do anything about it, why would he lie?" That was actually a pretty accurate evaluation of his character.

"But if he doesn't admit to it, he'll know we're looking," Royce said. "And he'll almost definitely make it harder for us to get any evidence."

"I can't believe this." Myles sank back down into his chair. "I can't believe this is a real conversation we're actually having right now."

"Believe it. You've spent too long seeing Dad's approval as the be-all, end-all purpose of your life." Royce's flat tone was starting to unnerve me a little. "No better way to move past that, I guess."

"Isn't it funny how the one of us who actually has his approval is the one who doesn't fucking want it?" Myles growled, quickly getting defensive. Knowing he was eager to start a fight with Royce and we wouldn't be able to work together if they were at each other's throats, I tried to step in.

"Royce, do you have an idea of how to look for proof? You know what kind of records Dad keeps."

Ignoring or unaware of Myles's glaring, he pinched the bridge of his nose as he considered. "I doubt he'll have it plainly stated anywhere, but I'm sure if I do some digging, I can find a list of who was working on the day of the 'accident.' After that, it's a matter of seeing who was being paid what, figuring out their individual jobs for the day..." He tilted his head back to look up at the ceiling. "It won't be a simple thing, but I think it's possible we could get some answers that way."

"Then let's start there."

"I still like the plan where we just go *talk* to him," Myles muttered.

But it turned out that wasn't an option.

I had been a little iffy about bringing Jill back to the house after my conversation about her with Dad. But he still hadn't come back from whatever job he'd gone out to do the day before. When Royce went to his office to try to look through his records, he wasn't there. Myles went to ask Rena while I asked around with the staff, but none of them had seen him at all that day.

"Rena says he didn't come home last night," Myles said, phone in hand and a scowl on his face as he came back from her room. "But he sent her a text earlier today. Just said 'something came up' and he'll be 'away on business for a while.'"

"That's weird." Royce's face was scrunched up in suspicion. "If it's business, I would expect him to share it with me, but I haven't heard from him since yesterday morning."

"Yeah, and he never sends texts," Myles agreed. "It's always phone calls or emails. What the hell is going on?"

"Do you think he knew you were suspicious?" Jill asked.

"Maybe he ran so he wouldn't have to explain himself to you?"

"Oh, if he doesn't want to explain, he won't," Royce assured her. "And he's not the kind of man who runs from anything. He's usually pretty easy for me to read, and I know this is definitely not like him."

"Well, him not being here just makes it easier to do your research, doesn't it?" she reasoned. "Maybe you can find the proof you need before he gets back, so when he does, you'll have him where you want him."

Myles suppressed a snicker. "Y'know, it's kind of too bad you guys are leaving. You would've made a great mafioso."

20

JILL

There was no one else in the visitation room when I got there, but that didn't help me to relax much. This would be my first time seeing my dad in private—more or less—since his arrest. The trial had taken some time, especially since Deron wasn't available to participate; after a full three months, he was still missing. The only reason I was there to visit was because my mom had asked me to go. I wasn't exactly looking forward to the conversation we were about to have.

The guards brought Dad in on the other side of the room, and he sat in the booth in front of me. A pang of guilt struck me when I saw how utterly exhausted he looked, but I tried to remind myself it was a result of his actions, not mine. I was only grateful that Deron had disappeared when he did; that meant there was no one to give an order for my dad to die there in jail. When he picked up the phone at his side, he managed a weak smile.

"Hi, sweetheart," he said. "It's good to see you."

"Yeah," I muttered into the receiver on my end. "You too. How is it here so far?"

"It's about what I expected. Lonely, more than anything. But I'd rather not talk about what goes on in here; I'm much interested in how you're doing. Your mother came by a few days ago, but she was crying so much she could hardly talk to me." His eyes drifted down toward the table he was resting against. "Is Annette still refusing to consider visiting me?"

"I mean, she does have reasons," I reminded him.

"I'll take that as a 'yes,'" he sighed.

"Yes, but I'm sure she won't feel that way forever."

"And what about you?" He met my eyes again, pleading for some kind of sympathy. I tried my best to feel some, but it wasn't easy. "Did you come here because you wanted to talk to me or because you felt obligated?"

"It's not because I'm obligated. I'm still deciding how I feel about all this," I said frankly. "You're still my dad. I still love you. But this isn't easy to look past."

He nodded slowly and, after a few seconds of silence, asked, "Can you give me an idea of how things are out there? I'm so cut off from everything and everyone in here, and I can't stand not knowing whether my family is all right." I knew the feeling.

"We're surviving," I said tersely. "'All right' might be a stretch. Mom hardly leaves the house, so I try to visit her whenever I can. Annette has been focusing harder on school. I'm finalizing the sale on the store soon."

His face fell even more. "I was afraid it might come to that."

"It was my choice. I tried to go back to work after your trial, but,"—I shook my head as I thought about how hollow the store had felt, how pointless it seemed to be there— "I couldn't. And Annette won't go anywhere near it, so I figured this was for the best."

"I'm sorry," he said quietly, for what seemed like the millionth time. Rather than telling him how hard it was to accept that apology, I just shrugged in response. "But what are you doing with all your time in that case? The store was everything to you before. Without it, you must have a lot of time freed up."

"Oh. Yeah, I guess." This was the part I was trying to avoid bringing up. Surely it wouldn't do him any good to hear it, right? But if he really wanted to know, I wasn't eager to keep any secrets. I took a deep breath and reminded myself I had no reason to fear his judgment anymore. "I've been spending a lot of time with Roger."

"Roger?" he repeated incredulously. "Roger Moretti? The one who kidnapped you? You can't be serious."

"I am. You know we were together before—"

"Ten years ago!"

"—And we still have feelings for each other. He's been incredibly supportive and helpful throughout all this." We could lean on each other during our respective family crises. Every day I felt closer to him. Being around all of the Moriettis again, as a family and not as captors, reminded me so much of all the time we'd spent together when we were younger. In some ways, I was actually happier than I'd been in a long time.

"Well, I'm sure he's seen it plenty of times," Dad muttered dismissively.

"I think you've pretty effectively lost your right to tell me who I can or can't date," I snapped right back.

"I'm just worried about you, Jill. I'm concerned for your safety. You know what he does for a living, what his family does. Those people are dangerous."

"You don't know as much about 'those people' as you think. They aren't all like Deron. In fact, most of them are actively trying not to be like him. They wouldn't hurt me or put me in danger. Besides, Roger isn't working for them anymore. He's just a part of the family, not the business."

"Those two things are inseparable when it comes to the Morettis." What made him think he knew them better than I did, I wasn't sure. "I'm telling you: trusting them is a mistake. People will start to think you're working for them, and no one will trust you. They'll ruin your life."

Astonished by his ignorance, I let out a scoff. "Dad, do you not realize how much publicity your trial got? How quickly I was labeled 'daughter of ex-mob killer'?"

It seemed like everyone in San Diego knew me and my family now. Those who weren't suspicious and judgmental were insufferable gossips instead. Brooke had no qualms about using our friendship—*former* friendship—to share all the detailed information the public wanted to know about the murderer's family, everything I'd told her in confidence over the past four years. It was doing wonders for her career. All sorts of rumors and speculation surrounded not only my relationship with my dad but my relationship with Roger. People were saying I was going to be the next Moretti queen. I was considered dangerous just like the rest of them. If that was what Dad meant by "ruin," I was already there.

"I'm not going to avoid being with the person I want just to save face. I'm done telling lies to keep other people comfortable. And that includes you."

"What about your own comfort?" he asked. "Because if you really think he would leave behind his entire life just for you—"

"I do believe that. You know why? Roger didn't lie to me for ten years straight thinking it was for my own good," I told him. "He hasn't lied to me once, in fact. And he would never kill another human being for money."

"You don't have to remind me what I've done, Jill. I haven't forgotten it for a single day since it happened," my dad seethed. "You've never been in the situation I was in. You don't understand what it's like to have no other choice."

"There's always another choice. Even if it's not the easiest one. Even if it means answering for your mistakes." I hung up the receiver and got to my feet, ignoring him as he called after me. The talk had gone about as well as I'd expected, and I couldn't keep sitting there trying to justify myself to him. I wouldn't.

Roger was waiting for me outside. "Hey. That didn't take long," he noted when he saw me. "Was he not in the mood to talk?"

"I said what I needed to." Stepping into his arms, I rested my head against his chest, and he held me without question. We'd talked plenty about how difficult this was going to be, so he understood that I needed the comfort. "Can we stop by the store for a minute? I don't want to go in or anything. I just want to see it."

"Sure. Whatever you want."

For the third time in the week since I'd found a buyer, we drove back to the store and parked outside. To say being there gave me mixed emotions would be an understatement. I did have a ton of great memories there, but I couldn't look at it anymore without thinking about what it had cost. It was too tied up in my dad's lies, Deron's ruthlessness, and our family's pain.

"You're sure you want to sell it?" Roger asked, looking up at the green Johnson Family Market sign on the front of the building. "When you talked about it before, you were so invested. All those plans you had for growing the chain. I mean, if it's about the money, we could help you out."

"I don't think another Moretti loan is going to do the trick," I said dryly.

"I'm not talking about a loan. I'm talking about us helping you with your business because you're..." He hesitated, aware of my similarly mixed feelings about being part of his family. "Because we care about you."

"It's not my business anymore. And expanding without earning it myself wouldn't mean anything. Besides, it's not like anyone is willing to do business with my family anymore." I laughed, but there was no real amusement behind it. "No. I'm ready to leave it behind and do something else with my life. Something I know is real and not built on a bunch of lies."

Roger leaned over and kissed my cheek, forcing me to smile genuinely. "I'm looking forward to seeing what you pick." His lips found my neck, and I suppressed a shiver from the warmth of his breath. "Whatever it is, I'm sure you'll end up killing it."

"Interesting choice of words," I laughed as I pushed him away. "Hey, you were talking to Royce earlier. Did he find anything new?" At the mention of this subject, Roger's good mood instantly faded.

"Kind of. He finally found Dad's financial records for the day Mom died. So we have some names, but that's it. There are still a lot of other details to sift through. And whoever he hired to do it probably won't be eager to confess." He frowned deeply, running a hand through his hair as he considered. "So we're not much closer to the proof we need —but at this point, I don't even know how much it matters. Dad's still missing, and I'm really starting to think it's not by choice."

"What do you mean?"

"It's not like him to just disappear for so long without

updating anyone," he explained. "He's such a micromanager he would be checking in on operations every other day. But Royce hasn't heard from him once, and it's been months. He hasn't contacted Rena either. So whatever's going on, I don't think it's business as usual. And I don't know what that implies for the rest of us."

"You think someone abducted him or something?" That was a difficult thought to accept, considering how much power Deron had in his position. Anyone who had *more* must have been a pretty high-profile character, which was a little disconcerting.

"I don't know," Roger sighed in frustration. "That's the problem. I have no idea what happened to him or what it implies for us. The last thing I want is to put you in danger—"

"But you recognize that that's not your decision to make," I finished for him with a smile. "And you know I'm not going to let a little danger keep me away from you."

"Don't worry, I know better than to exclude you from anything without your permission. I've been thinking it might be good for you to learn some self-defense, actually. You're plenty convincing if someone's willing to let you talk, but you might not always have that option," he reasoned. And it was a logical thought.

"Okay, but don't think you're going to draw me into the family business gradually that way." The teasing smile on my lips made it clear this was a joke. Although to be honest, I was still a little unsure on the subject.

I thought sometimes about what Myles had told me, that I would have been a good fit for the job. The loyalty I felt to Roger and his brothers. How easy it was for me to dismiss sympathy and repay ruthlessness with more ruthlessness. My dad had done some horrible things for reasons he thought were valid. Who was to say I wouldn't end up doing the same? What I told my dad was true: Roger hadn't been involved in any jobs or business negotiations for the past three months. We were staying at the house and working closely with Royce and Myles.That was just until we found Deron and paid him back for Latasha's death. And that was a valid reason. Wasn't it?

"Family, yes. Business, no," Roger agreed with a smirk. Nodding to the store, he asked, "You ready to head home?" Home. With him. I still liked that.

"Sure."

21

ROGER

Six months. Dad had never been gone for six months straight before, not for my entire life. We'd pretty much exhausted every resource we could think of, and every day, it seemed more like we would only find him when he wanted to be found—or whoever had taken him wanted it. I still couldn't think why anyone would go to the trouble of *taking* him in the first place. Just one more unanswered question on a frustratingly long list.

Our extended family and all our business contacts had started to panic a little, They thought Dad's disappearance would be the end of the Morettis as a group. They couldn't function completely on their own. There needed to be someone on the throne, to give orders and maintain control. After the scare we had about the family's stability, it was even easy for people to get spooked.

Even though everyone knew he was the best man for the job and multiple people had personally asked him to take it, Royce was still balking at the idea of claiming Dad's position for himself. He didn't want all that power or the reputation that came with it. He didn't want to sentence Whitney to life as a boss's daughter and all that entailed. He didn't even want to be *involved* in the family's work, much less to run it. He and I had that in common.

Maybe we should've been grateful that Myles was willing to step up. When he proposed it, Royce and I were both a little unsure. It was possible that Myles being the one in charge would be even worse than not having a boss at all. But, like he pointed out, having someone in charge would make everyone else more comfortable. And there were certain privileges and resources that came with the title, things we couldn't access while we were still just "heirs"— things that might help us find Dad or get answers about Mom's death.

"Are you going to do it?" Myles asked, looking between the two of us. "Because if you're not, we literally have no other options. We don't know when or if Dad's coming back. We can't expect him to show up and solve this for us. Meaning one of us needs to take the job. And I know why you're both looking at me like that, but I know I can do this."

"Are you sure?" Royce looked unconvinced. "It's not an easy job to do, and you don't know all the ins and outs."

"So teach me," Myles countered. "Tell me everything you know about running the business, and I'll put it into action. Nobody's going to question if I'm committed to the job. What I lack in experience, I'll make up for in charisma." He grinned, obviously excited about the prospect. He was still only twenty-three, but there had probably been younger bosses in history. "And most importantly: I'm *willing* to do it. You two aren't. Doesn't that kind of settle it?" I glanced at Royce, hoping he would either persuade Myles otherwise or agree to give him lessons. Without them, he was going to get himself killed, and quick.

"Okay," Royce said, nodding slowly. "If you'll actually

listen to me, I'll support you from the sidelines. But listen. I'm not going to do the job for you, and I'm not going to be your advisor forever. Once you're okay on your own—"

"Then I'll be fine with you stepping back. Come on, guys, try to have a little confidence in me. Or at least pretend to. It'll work out. You'll see."

He made the announcement the next week, calling all the most important players into the conference room and giving a well-rehearsed speech about taking responsibility and thinking about the family's future. Between his slicked-back hair, his confident body language, and the way he easily talked his way out of any objections that were raised, it really was like watching a younger version of Dad. I wanted to believe he would turn out better, but I couldn't help worrying, anyway. Maybe with Royce and me keeping an eye on him, he'd have an easier time thinking about his actions before he made any more rash decisions.

After the meeting, once all his guests had left, he dropped the Dignified Heir routine and whooped, and high fived Royce, who had been giving him lessons since our first conversation. As apprehensive as he'd been about the whole thing, he was still smiling like he was proud of Myles's progress.

"Don't get cocky," he warned. "It's only going to get harder from here."

"Yeah," Myles agreed, "and I'm gonna keep crushing it."

"I guess the meeting went well?" Rena came into the living room from her sewing room, leading Jill and Whitney behind her. The three of them had been spending more and more time together lately for some reason, maybe because Royce and I were distracted trying to solve the deal with our dad. And I felt like it was good for Jill. Annette had gotten steadily more distant over the past few months, her mom was so depressed she hardly talked, and Brooke was definitely not a part of her life anymore. So it was a relief that she had at least *some* other women in her life to talk to.

"Surprisingly, yeah, it did." I reached up to muss Myles's carefully arranged hair, and he groaned as he squirmed away from me. "He didn't fuck up even one single part of it."

"Hey, you better watch your mouth," he said, quickly drawing back up to his full height and giving me an exaggerated glare. "You know who I am? You know what I can do to you?"

I rolled my eyes. "Save it for somebody who never saw you cry over a dead goldfish."

Before he could answer, the doorbell rang. Royce was closest, so he went to answer it. "Were we missing someone at the meeting? I didn't think—" He stopped when he opened the door and saw who was standing there. The woman was around thirty, no taller than 5' 4", with dark brown skin and black hair pulled into several shining braids. Royce and Whitney recognized her at the same time.

"Margot."

"Mummy!" Whits zipped across the room to meet her, and Margot caught her in a fierce hug.

"Hello, my love! I've missed you so much!" Her accent was a lot more noticeable than Whitney's. She planted several kisses in her daughter's thick curls before getting to her feet, still keeping hold of Whitney's hand. When she looked up, her smile faded. "Royce. Nice to see you." Her chilly tone said otherwise.

"What..." He swallowed hard, visibly shell-shocked. "What are you doing here?"

"I invited her," Jill said brightly, coming over to my side and giving Margot a little wave.

"Jill! It's so nice to finally meet you in person." They hugged, and Royce exchanged a stupefied glance with me.

"How did you invite her?" I asked, lost as to how they would have even met. Had she sought out Margot's contact information just to make this reunion happen?

"We've been talking for a few months now," Jill said with a shrug, as if this was a totally casual thing. "She knows what it's like trying to deal with a Moretti who can't get out from under his dad's thumb, so we have a couple of things in common. Since Deron isn't here at the moment and I know how much she and Whitney have been missing each other, it made sense to me that she should come and join us here."

"I should've come back straight away when you did," Margot agreed, carefully arranging Whitney's hair. "If being in the middle of this horrid mess is what it takes to stay close to my child, I suppose it can't be helped."

"Maggie," Royce started, but she ignored him.

"Anyway, I'm going to keep Jill company while—" She stopped as Jill quickly shook her head. She glanced at me, then back at Jill, and hissed, "Have you not told him?"

"Told me what?"

"Holy shit." Myles's eyes were so wide I thought they'd pop out of his head. "You're preggers!"

"*What?*" I snapped back toward Jill. "Are you...?"

She smiled sheepishly. "Surprise?" For a second, my brain practically short-circuited, and I had no idea how to respond. *Jill is... which means we're... and I'm going to be...*

"Holy shit. Babe, holy shit!" I grabbed her and spun her around, then kissed her hard.

"Is that a positive reaction?" she laughed as she pulled away.

"Yes!" So much for her birth control, but it wasn't like I was complaining. "This is amazing. This is fucking incredible!" I wanted to be mad she had told someone else before me, but I was too ecstatic over the news to complain about any part of it. If someone had asked me before that moment how I felt about having kids, I would've been unsure. But now that it was a reality, I couldn't have possibly been happier.

"Wow. Congratulations," Royce said, shaking out of his stupor to come over and slap me on the back.

"... Seven, eight, now nine," Myles was saying. "This family's getting huge."

All I could focus on was Jill. Keeping her close against me, I muttered, "I'm going to make sure this baby grows up happy and comfortable and safe. Not involved in any of this—"

"Hey!" Myles called.

"—Any of this mafia bullshit." I shot him a brief glare before turning my eyes back to her. "I promise. I love you. God, I love you."

She stood up on her toes to kiss me again. "I love you too. And I'm going to hold you to that promise."

9 798631 905900